The Girl from Home

By

AGNES KAY-E

This novel is entirely a work of fiction. The names, characters, and incidents portrayed in it are the work of the author's imagination. Any resemblance to actual persons, living or dead, events or localities is entirely coincidental.

978 978 972 400 0 (Paperback)
978 978 972 401 7 (Ebook)
978 191 637 100 2 (Hardback)

Cover design by James, GoOnWrite.com

To

All who believe in love and forgiveness.

"To truly love: one, must first learn to forgive one's self."
– Agnes Kay-E

"It's in you to create your happiness.
And in you to find your happy place."

- Agnes Kaye-E

CHAPTER 1

Soon after they got to the edge of the overgrown garden, Kelechi counted the snails they had picked and sighed. It wasn't enough. She'd wanted to get enough for her grandmother and Mrs Barine, her godmother.

Johnson murmured suddenly, "let's make a pact."

"Like an oath or something?" Kelechi asked, uninterested in another dare.

"Yes," he retorted matter-of-factly.

"I'm not doing any blood oath or anything else o!" she responded in her most serious voice.

He wrinkled his nose. "No! I mean, like a promise."

"Then call it a promise," Kelechi mumbled, kicking off the twig that had stuck to her shoe.

"Let's promise," Johnson paused and waited until she caught up to him. "to find each other when we get lost."

"You don come o!" Kelechi retorted mournfully.

"When you think I'm acting strange or get

uncomfortable, you switch to Pidgeon English."

"Do I? I do?" Kelechi asked and hissed when she could no longer see the lantern fires of the other searchers. "Abeg, we're going to be late, and I'll end up without enough snails. I promised mama o!"

"Kechi, this is serious o!"'

"Everything is serious with you. I don't like it when you call me 'Kechi'."

"But your grandmother does."

"My grandmother," she emphasized.

"Fine, about what I said." He paused dramatically.

"Why will a big boy like you get lost eh?"

Ignoring her tone, he continued. "Not loss as in finding-a-street-lost," Johnson stamped his feet when they got to the tarred road to remove mud from his shoes.

Kelechi joined him and impatiently did the same as she spoke. "You know something, you are an old man in a young body. How many times have you reincarnated, abeg?"

"I don't know what you're talking about," Johnson defended.

"Exactly. Why would I come and find you when you get lost?"

"Because you love me?" Johnson curiously asked.

Kelechi scoffed.

"Promise me."

"Promise me first," Kelechi muttered and carried on walking towards the others. The snails weren't going to wait for them, and neither were the other searchers ahead of them.

"Kelechi, stop! This is important."

Kelechi grumbled. "I promise that when you get lost, I'll go in search of you and keep searching until I find you."

"Okay, thank you! Shall we?" Kelechi asked and started walking.

Johnson blocked her path. "No, say your own."

Kelechi repeated what he'd said and gestured.

"Till death do us part," Johnson continued.

Kelechi pulled back. "Ha! What if I want to marry someone else?"

Johnson's eyes narrowed, his heart racing. "Do you want to?"

Kelechi indignantly glared at him. "I don't know!" she'd sighed and added solemnly. "The future is too big."

"Kechi, the future is now," he said softly with a smile and cupped her face, his gaze hopeful as he repeated. "Till death do us part."

Kelechi, wanting the conversation to end, obliged him. "Till death do us part."

"For better or worse."

"For better or worse," Kelechi sighed, watching him. He had been a little withdrawn

and lost in thought lately. Concerned, but not wanting to prolong his need to keep talking, she didn't query him.

Johnson stopped walking and waited for her to catch up.

Worry finally caught up with her, and she asked, "Is everything okay?"

"Yes, and I'm fine."

She squinted at him. "Are you sure?"

"Yes nawh."

Kelechi touched his forehead, apart from the beads of sweat, his temperature was normal.

"Girlie, I'm okay."

"Oh, it's no longer 'Kechi'?"

Johnson chuckled. "Don't be like that nawh."

"I am o!" Kelechi murmured hurriedly walked ahead of him. But he caught up with her and tickled her until she begged him to stop.

Kelechi snickered and returned to her surroundings. *So far from home*, she thought and sighed, staring at her wedding band before looking around the crowded airport. She was not one for travelling, but she was making an exception. She'd promised. What is the worst that could happen?

CHAPTER 2

Kelechi tentatively pressed the bell and waited. She frowned at the now wet paper - it was the right address - she pressed the bell again. A woman in an oversized shirt and dishevelled red hair opened the door. Cold, tired, and not ready to knock on another door, she greeted the lady.

"I'm Kelechi. I'm looking for Mr ....," she said and began to cough.

The woman looked inquisitively at her.

"Nwunye'm!" Johnson exclaimed as he scrambled for the door, then made slow, hesitant steps towards the women at the entrance and finally came to a halt between Stella and Kelechi.

"Come in, come in," he quickly said, scratching his head, his chest, and finally tucked his hands in his pocket and repeated the process while he led Kelechi in. He promptly unhooked her large knapsack and gestured to the sofa bed.

The woman with the dishevelled hair thinned her lips and frowned at Johnson, crossed her arms, and watched them, a funny expression on her face. Johnson hadn't noticed, but the woman had not moved an inch from the door.

Kelechi looked at the mussy fussy state of the room and sat on the edge of a tiny sofa by the wall.

"What may I offer you?" Johnson asked, vigorously rubbing his arm.

"Nothing. I'm fine. I just wanted to -"

"Hold that thought!" he said in a lilting voice. He went away and returned with Stella then cleared his throat. "Kelechi-mo, I would like you to meet Stella..."

With a broad smile, Stella stretched out a hand. "Hello, and welcome."

Kelechi smiled thinly.

"What would you like?" Johnson asked. "We've got..."

"Nothing." Kelechi retorted as she removed her soaked trainers.

"I want to... I'm sorry, I didn't get your name." Stella blinked; her curiosity piqued.

"I'm Kelechi Umeh," Kelechi replied with wide-eyed innocence. She was about to ask, 'and who might you be?'.

"Is Mama okay?" Johnson impatiently cut in.

Kelechi nodded, curious to know who the woman with them was, especially as the woman didn't leave.

"Papa?" Johnson asked, prodding her to keep talking.

Kelechi nodded, returning her gaze to the white

red-haired lady behind him.

"What of..."

"Is this an interrogation?" Stella cut in. "Your sister just got in!"

Kelechi choked and coughed. "What?" Kelechi wheezed.

Johnson and Stella sighed in tandem, then Stella looked at the time. "Why don't I go to the party so you two can catch up?" She asked a little too eagerly and quickly shrug out of the oversized shirt then pulled on a timid, shimmering silver dress that barely covered her buttocks. Kelechi blinked as she watched the strange woman pull on a long boot and gawkishly searched for the other pair.

"JJ, order dinner, will you?" With that, she left the sitting room.

Johnson massaged Kelechi's back until she recovered. She began to cough again. The sitting room smelled of dirty laundry mixed with varied fragrances. Suspecting that her coughing had something to do with the stale smells in the room, she held her breath and lowered her head into her snood. With her face set in a grimace, Kelechi looked around and shuddered.

Dresses, shirts, shoes, and stringy-looking things littered the small sitting room like little islands on the Pacific. Dust coated everything. Her eyes widened when she saw something that looked like mushrooms on a half-full plate of food by the wine glasses. She looked around in search of a bin as her skin rapidly began to crawl. It was a wonder that she hadn't sneezed, and of course, just then, she did.

Johnson tried to soothe her, but she brushed his hand away. She was sure something was off, apart from the fact that she'd just discovered her husband was dirty.

Stella returned, hair wrapped up in a ponytail, her face made-up to suit a barbie doll, her earrings as large as saucers. To Kelechi's horror, Stella sat in one of the stinking mess to pull on the second boot.

Kelechi blinked; England was an entirely different world indeed. She twisted her mouth, wondering if she would be able to cope? Then she remembered what her cousin, Barinem, had told her: 'it is like Lagos but with constant light.'

Johnson averted his gaze each time Kelechi's eyes queried.

"Keleeshi, I hope you're staying?" Stella drawled, roused herself, wrapped her arms around Johnson, and passionately kissed him.

Kelechi's mouth hung open, her eyes wide, her body frozen.

Stella may have sensed Johnson's discomfort, but did not refer to it. She patted his chest. "My husband will take care of you."

CHAPTER 3

Kelechi stared wide-eyed at Stella's hurried exit. She slapped her cheek to wake up from the nightmare. She pointed, gestured and shook her head, and laughed hysterically until she couldn't anymore, then she turned to pinch herself to wake up. She tried to get up, but her legs had turned to jelly.

Johnson went on his knees immediately after he heard the door click shut.

Kelechi stared morosely at Johnson as tears began to stream down her face.

Johnson clasped his hand in prayer as he began to plead.

Kelechi felt like she'd been thrown into the sea without limbs with no way to keep the waters out of her mouth. She flicked her thumbs and middle fingers several times, wishing it was a dream. She now understood why Barinem was reluctant to tell her where her husband lived. Why his friends never visited his parents when she was in the house. She looked him over and shuddered as she tried to figure out what she felt. Shock? Shame?

She shook her head. It was stupidity, waiting for nine years. Nine years of faithfully waiting for him. Her sheer stupidity

"I've been such a fool! Your parents knew, didn't they? Now it makes sense," she nodded as she finally got up, still clicking her fingers. "Why? So, I was a pawn for your bruised ego just because I refused to sleep with you before marriage? Was I a charity case because I had no family?"

"No," he crawled towards her. "You were the love of my life."

"Were." she sniggered. Seeing her husband on his knees, begging, irritated her, but it wasn't worse than his betrayal. "Thanks for letting me know that I'm your past."

"It's not like that." He pleaded, and the doorbell chimed, "Who is that?" he asked, angry at the interruption but somewhat relieved. He went to answer the door and returned with a bag of what Stella had ordered. As soon as he got to the sitting room, he set the bag down and moved close to Kelechi. She turned away at the same time and picked her bag up.

Kelechi gently cleared her throat. "Show me to my room."

"Nwunye'm (my wife), let me explain," he started and looked hopefully at her.

"Nwunye onye (whose wife)? Please go and meet Nwunye gi before she goes far o!"

"Imagu nu (you know), no one can take your place," he assured her as he reached out for her.

Kelechi recoiled, then came forward and pushed him with such force he fell back onto the chair. Impatiently, she opened the door behind her and discovered that it was the kitchen. She walked around him. Outside the sitting room were three other doors; one was the exit, by her right the bathroom. When she entered the room, she choked.

"How can you dwell in this mess?"

"I was thinking..."

"I'm not leaving this house!" Kelechi warned. *If you thought I would leave you with someone else, you're highly mistaken.*

Johnson scratched his head. He tried to mirror her movement while avoiding her gaze. Finally, he pulled and held her in place facing him. "I had no choice. My Visa had expired. Please understand."

Kelechi stared at him in horror, whispering. "You're using her!"

"I don't have a choice," he murmured sternly.

"You did. Why didn't you just come back?" She asked, surprised at how desperately she wanted, needed an answer.

"To what?" he queried.

Stung, Kelechi opened her mouth and shut it.

He paced, swinging his hands. "I'm not from an influential family. There's no job waiting for me back home. How am I supposed to take care of you and my parents and the rest of the family?"

"We agreed to cut our coats to our size! Or did the weather erase that?"

"I tried to save, but one problem after the other stunted that plan."

"Excuses! Well, I told you so," she snapped.

"Were you expecting us to have kids in that dump?"

Kelechi frowned, annoyed that she wasn't getting the answer she'd hoped for. "Are you done?"

Johnson grimaced.

She let out an exasperated sigh, shaking her head. "That so-called dump is what your parents were left with when they decided to train you abroad. That dump is where your parents raised you. That dump is where you abandoned your so-called wife."

"Stop!"

She sniggered. "I'm sleeping in this room."

"If I say no?"

She scoffed and spun to glare at him. "I'm not naïve! I'm done playing the little girl you met fetching and selling firewood. You chose to pay my dowry and wed me. You also chose to leave me behind with the promise of returning in four years. You chose to move me into your parents' house, the so-called dump. You even chose to make me their carer."

Johnson was about to respond, but she held up a hand as she tried to catch her breath. "I have now made my choice, to be by your side, to be a dutiful wife and mother to your children. By God, not even you will stand in my way!"

Johnson's shoulder slumped. "Stella cannot know about this, please."

"For fear of bigamy, *okwaya (is that it)*?"

Johnson nodded, unsure of what she understood.

"Very well, most men in Nigeria have more than one wife."

"So, you will stay in the sitting room." He scrambled around for a shirt. "I will go and buy a duvet right away."

Kelechi laughed maniacally. "What a joke!"

"But..." he scratched his head and mumbled. "What do I tell Stella?"

Kelechi hissed and walked out of the room. By the time she returned from the kitchen, he'd left the house. She shuddered at the mess in the room and wondered where she would start; there was no way she was going to sleep in the room as it was.

She'd been exhausted from two days without sleep. She lowered her head and saw a sliver of green lace in the shape of a catapult around her foot and tried to free her foot. In the struggle, it flew through the air and landed on her face. Her repulsion of the assault caused her to retch where she stood. She quickly opened the windows and ran into the kitchen to fetch what she could use to clean it. Finding nothing, she ran to the toilet.

Johnson returned an hour later. He caught sight of Kelechi cleaning and withdrew because cleaning was her solace, whether she was happy or sad, and the circumstance they were in wasn't a pleasant one. Unable to help himself, he turned to the bedroom, but his courage faltered. He would give her the world, he decided, but not now. She just had to be patient with him.

He leaned on the door then raised a brow, remembering that she had only come in with a knapsack; this meant that he could buy her a few clothes. He didn't know her size or if she would accept it. But he had to try.

He glanced at his watch and set out again. This time, in a hurry. He hoped he could find Kelechi something she'd like before the shops closed. He squinted at his credit cards and wiped away the tears that trickled down his face. He pulled out the one he'd gotten in a false name from the wallet and tossed the wallet on the settee.

On his way out of the living room, he accidentally tilted Kelechi's knapsack and saw a memo pad. Curious, he sneakily peered at it as he listened for her. It had a list:

Collared shirt
Turtleneck sweaters
Pencil skirt
Tights
Knee-length boots
Winter jacket
Undies

At the word 'undies', his heart raced, and he shook his head vigorously. He flipped through it and saw another list and squinted at the heading: *KNOW THIS*. It read:

They love to talk about the weather
They love tea the way we love food
Stand on the right, i.e. at the road, look right to left
Best not to travel when big football teams are playing, it's less safe
Taxi phone numbers
999, 112, - emergency number
(101 and 111 - non-emergency number)?
Never jump the queue.

Johnson chuckled at the last sentence, knowing she never did but was keen to find out why she wrote it down. At the end of the list was a string of words starting with three asterisks, about cheese rolling, black pudding throwing, and duck racing, followed by Uber, YouTube, and Netflix in brackets.

He made a mental note to use the awareness of what they were to his advantage. He had to be quick, too; one thing he was sure of was the fact that she was resourceful. One of the few things Stella was incapable of. He reprimanded himself, Stella was capable in everything but being a wife.

Kelechi appraised her work: the room was now devoid of clutter, and the dust minimal, but she wouldn't be able to sleep in it without further stripping. She gaped at the colour-coded pile she'd made and decided to put the first set in the wash. She almost stumbled over something in the hallway and realised it was the duvet her husband had promised to buy.

Annoyed, she kicked it out of the way, but it rolled back as if in silent defiance. She raised a curious brow when her husband didn't say anything. So, she feigned disinterest as she took the first batch of clothes to the kitchen. Seeing that he wasn't there, she quickly started the wash and rushed to the toilet. Angry tears streaked down her face. She wanted to crush him, but she didn't have it in her. What would people say? She scoffed, wondering when she began to care about people's opinions. It begged the question of how much she'd changed and if it was indeed a good thing.

She couldn't dwell on her pain at the moment. She had cakes to bake - a heart-shaped cake and a three-tier birthday cake. She'd given her word, plus she needed the money now more than ever. She'd have to go back to Barinem's place and figure out her next move from there.

Although satisfied that the room was clean, she was hesitant in sleeping in the bed her husband had shared with another woman. Embarrassed and a little harassed, she continued cleaning until it was almost midnight. The fact that there were no clean sheets made it easier to stay away from the bed. But by the time she was done baking the final cake, she was too drowsy to be choosy. She decided to use the new duvet and found a new sheet in the bag. Without sparing enough time to cover the duvet, she crawled into bed and dozed off.

Johnson returned a lot later than planned. He'd seen a friend who owed him with a new girl and decided to cash in on the opportunity and was lucky. Glad for it, he bought a few extra things for Kelechi. When he got into the room, he found her sleeping fully clothed. He removed her shoes and tights; seeing her bare was quite stimulating so much so he wanted to get her out of the many clothes.

Startled by Stella's raised voice, he quickly got off the bed, pulled the duvet over Kelechi, and left the room. In his hurry, he stumbled over something in the hallway. He scrambled to get to the socket and tripped again, falling into the settee. He groaned. The stark difference between the bedroom and the sitting room was staggering. The bedroom was now spotless, cleaner than when he'd moved in two and a half years ago.

He picked the clothes that lay on the ground, scurried to the kitchen and exclaimed. He gawked at the transformation then look up at the time and gawked again, baffled. It was almost five a.m. He guffawed in surprise, comprehending the fact that he'd been out for a long time. Seeing the time, he became annoyed because Stella was supposed to have returned at least four hours earlier. It was the third time in the same week that she'd disappeared on him. He didn't mind her night-outs, but she was like a child with sweets.

Sighing, he opened the washing machine. It had clothes in it, and so did the laundry basket. Awed at the amount of work Kelechi had done in such a short period, albeit hours, he spread the clothes and pondered.

Back in university, he had huge prospects and almost didn't take a job. In a way, he was grateful for his parents' illness, without which he wouldn't have earned the experience needed to work with the architectural firm that had made him associate. *Three months to go,* he sighed, shaking his head. He was so close to becoming a partner in the firm and couldn't let his emotions be frayed.

He hadn't told Stella yet, knowing how extravagant she was. He was still crumbling under the debt she'd incurred in his name. He'd always been careful with his credit to secure a mortgage, and she destroyed it in one go. For a while, she'd been shredding the letters from the credit card companies. Sometimes he suspected that she squandered the money because he'd been adamant about wanting kids.

"This silk dress is the price of all my wardrobe, and she didn't even wear it to the gala," he moaned. He tossed the silk dress down. After a few deep breaths, he bent down to pick it, grimacing as he did. He had no idea Stella was close until she wrapped her arms around him.

Irritated, he unhooked her arms then turned her wrist to show her the time.

In response, she harrumphed and burped.

"It's five AM," he emphasized.

"Come on," She sighed and made her way to the toilet bowl. "I wanted you to catch up with your sister."

He cringed at the mess she'd made and stopped spreading the clothes briefly to help her.

"Where have you been?" He asked, propping her.

"Don't take that tone with me!"

Johnson grinned, knowing that she was pretending to be drunk. In a few hours, she'd call in sick then tell him she couldn't stand the noise of Watling Avenue and run off to Portia's only to return at night. He made a mental note to call his colleague to cover for him so he could talk to Kelechi when Stella was away.

"I need you," Stella moaned.

He brushed her off and left for the kitchen. Not wanting to fight with Kelechi, he stacked the cakes and tucked them in the oven.

"JJ?" Stella cried.

He turned to leave the kitchen and almost bumped into Stella, who was already naked.

She sniggered, burped, and repeated. "I need you."

He was beginning to feel uneasy, especially with Kelechi in the room, just a wall away. Yet...

Kelechi woke up with a fright. She thought she'd heard screaming. Acquainted with her surroundings, she slanted her head, and a bag caught her eyes. There was a sticky note attached to it, peeling it, she wrinkled her nose.

While she made a quick prayer, she heard the click of the lock and assumed it was the bathroom, so she hurried to the kitchen. Her husband was not in the sitting room. The look of satisfaction on Stella's face gave her the impression of what had just taken place, and she was glad she had slept through it even though a part of her brimmed with jealousy.

Disgusted, she decided she was never going to clean the sitting room. She'd rather his second wife did it for him.

CHAPTER 4

"Good morning," Kelechi murmured from where she stood by the sink.

Stella reciprocated and gasped, blinked, and licked her lips. The kitchen glistened; piles of plastic plates and cups shielding its ceramic counterparts were all gone. She innocuously picked up a mug and poured herself a cup of coffee and began to sip it. The coffee tasted great, which meant the kettle, and the coffee filter had been descaled.

Flushed with embarrassment, she swallowed, scalding her tongue and tried not to squeal. She had planned to teach her sister-in-law how to use the cooker and the washing machine. But the oven was on, two pots were cooking on the cooktop, and the washing machine was churning. She inhaled slowly, savouring the smell that had engulfed the kitchen; vanilla, cinnamon, and lemon, amongst other delicious and strange aromas. Unsure of another way to connect with her sister-in-law, she quickly left the kitchen, and with great reluctance, she went out of the house.

Kelechi sniggered. Slanting her head, she saw Stella leave and returned to what she was doing.

If they think I'll cook for them, then they have another thing coming. I'm going to prove to that ignoramus that I'm always better dressed than this. Guilt tinged a part of her mind, reminding her that Stella was innocent of Johnson's action.

She peered at the children on the street and cursed the fact that the kitchen window faced the road but couldn't resist watching them either. A boy pulled his sister's collar while another child much taller cautioned him. She blinked back tears when she could no longer hear them and went back to washing.

She checked the last cake and nodded her satisfaction, then cleared the worktop to start decorating. She hummed and worked her hands like she was weaving then removed the cupcakes from the oven when she heard a knock. Although she ignored it, she was curious to see who it was. She quickly scrambled for the bedroom and peered through the window.

It was a tall girl. It was hard to determine her age, plus they all looked the same to her, except this one, like Stella, had red hair and wore red boots. The red boots reminded Kelechi that she needed to get herself a pair. She hadn't heard the door being opened, but the barking dog drew her attention back to the window, where she saw Stella and the red-haired lady on the opposite side of the road. She watched them hug and blow kisses and shrugged. She had not seen Stella return.

She reprimanded herself for being distracted and let out a determined sigh.

"TJ has to put curtains on this window as soon as possible," she mused loudly to keep her thoughts at bay.

She opened the fridge and wedged it with one of the high stools. It was empty except for the icing sugar decorations of butterflies and flowers. She groaned; she had made white butterflies and pink flowers and nothing blue. She bit her lip, thinking of how she was going to solve the problem. While pondering on a solution, she decided to prepare the cake for Simisola's mother.

As she melted the chocolate, she heard the shower and knew her husband was up. She exhaled slowly as her heart began to constrict. Baffled at her reaction, she shook her head.

"What is wrong with me? It doesn't make sense to want a man who has been with another woman."

She sighed ruefully. "But he is my husband."

She is his wife also, her thought sniped.

Scratching her head, she scoffed. "I was his

wife first!"

But he is with her! He has known her in a way that he hasn't known you in all your years together.

Her shoulders fell at that truth. She tried to rely on the feeling that Stella had lured him into marrying her, but they seemed coordinated, complimenting each other.

"Nwunye'm," Johnson called. "You've got a call o!"

How dare he call me Nwunye'm? Kelechi thought and yanked the phone from him.

"Hello?" She cheerfully asked and frowned. "So, what am I supposed to do with it? Of course, I have already baked it. Why give your word if you don't mean it?" Kelechi stared at the phone after the line went dead. She gritted her teeth then let out a wistful sigh. The world seemed out to get her.

Just then, another call came in. "Hello?"

"No vex o. Did I catch you at a bad time?"

"Simisola?" Kelechi queried.

"Yes nawh! Who else will own a sexy voice such as mine?" Simisola jovially asked.

Kelechi smiled. "Thanks for lightening my mood."

"How did it go with your husband?"

Kelechi hissed, a long hiss.

"That bad?"

She exhaled despairingly. "Long story!"

"Yarn me nawh!" Simisola pleaded.

"Another time, *abeg* (please). When are you picking up the cake?"

"Oh, very soon! I need the car, so I'm waiting for Isaac. Abeg, don't charter taxi o! I want the taxi money so I will go with you to drop the big cake."

Kelechi sniggered. "They no longer want it o!"

"What!? I hope they paid you o!"

"For where!"

"Hey! God will judge them o!"

"Abeg, pay me your own so that God will not judge you too."

"Ha! It's true o. Me and my big mouth, I will bring it with me. Hold on, what colour is the big cake?"

"Blue, pink and white."

"Na lie!"

"You say wetin?"

"Those are my mother's favourite colours. Hold on. How much is it?"

"Nwunye'm, I want to talk to you," Johnson cut in.

Kelechi stared daggers at him and said into the phone, "same as we'd agreed," she said and wrinkled her nose, ending the call. She crossed her arms, stared coolly at Johnson.

Johnson cleared his throat a few too many times. "It's about the sleeping arrangement."

She hissed and gritted her teeth again, scolding herself. *You're out of options! Tread softly.*

The doorbell chimed. A knock followed it.

He scratched his head. "Can we at least talk about it?"

She hissed again and brushed past him. She looked through the bedroom window and saw an obscured silhouette of a person as it was hidden in a hooded jacket.

She glanced around the room until her eyes fell on the shopping bag. She emptied the shopping bags on the bed. Relieved, she picked out the towel and began to undress. She heard her husband welcome the person and rushed to the bedroom door.

Johnson got to the door before her, shut it, and made his way into the sitting room. He and his guest immediately switched to speaking in Igbo language. Kelechi knew the owner of the other voice, Maurice.

"Ol'boy, you know your oyibo wife is untidy like you. Why not hire a cleaner?"

"She doesn't have time, and she isn't untidy," Johnson defended.

Kelechi sniggered but suspected that Johnson said it to stop Maurice from saying anything suspicious. Because she could no longer hear them, she suspected they had entered the kitchen. She saw it as her cue to go into the bathroom. She could hear them clearly even with the shower being on and was also shocked at the lies that spewed from Maurice's mouth. She'd always known that he wasn't a trustworthy person the minute he asked her out knowing full well that she was married to his best friend. She was glad that Johnson hadn't said anything to Maurice about her being in the house.

Seeing that he would be expecting Stella, she planned to attend the party, if only to know the people who knew about Stella and those who were in support of her husband's action Nodding as she planned, she cleaned the bathroom.

A knock on the bedroom door surprised her. Hearing the click of its hinges as it was being opened gave her good reason to ensure she locked it when she was in there. She had to find its key as soon as possible.

"Ol'boy, did you hire someone to clean this room? Pesin dey this house? Baaaad buy!" Maurice gyrated with a knowing smile.

"I didn't know you knew how it looked before now," Johnson said, trying to change the topic and chuckled. Johnson frowned at Maurice's shocked expression. What he had to discover now was if he had slept with Stella. The Maurice he knew didn't respect boundaries. He appraised his friend in a new light. *Did something happen between Maurice and Stella?* This question had once plagued him before when Stella was obsessed with knowing the extent of their friendship.

Maurice feigned a shrug. “Nah, it’s just different from the sitting room. Anyway, your wife no dey so hail am for me. Make una show o!”

Johnson made up his mind right then to keep an eye on Maurice. He knew Stella didn’t understand the value of fidelity, and he was going to tolerate all he could until he had reached partnership. He liked the fact that she wasn’t faithful because it would ease his mind when he was done with her. Looking at the clothes on the bed, he wondered if the Kelechi he’d left in Nigeria was the same one in his house. However, he was plagued by her reaction to his having another wife, albeit by proxy, as it was supposed to be a sham. He’d told her in his letters, and she’d consented. Perhaps, it was because he wasn’t supposed to be sleeping with her. *Women!*

The doorbell chimed again. Thinking it was Maurice, he didn’t bother to check.

Raising a brow, he asked. “Simi?”

“Yes,” she nodded. “You must be Thomas.”

He cleared his throat. “I’d prefer Johnson.”

“Johnson,” Simisola murmured. “Is Kelechi in? I’m here for the cakes.”

He slanted his head, hearing the shower, he nodded. "Of course, come in," he said, stepping aside. "Kelechi is indisposed. I can help you with carrying the cake."

"I'd be grateful," Simisola said in a small voice and waited.

Johnson waited too.

"Sorry," Simisola laughed nervously and dug around her bag. "Here."

Johnson counted the money and nodded; he didn't know how much she was expected to pay. He went into the kitchen and brought out the brown, chocolate-covered heart-shaped cake and handed it over to her. then disappeared and returned with the bigger cake. "Lead the way," he murmured.

Johnson returned a few minutes later, to find Kelechi in the room. Engulfed with the thought of her being naked, he hurried to the kitchen to drink water, and his stomach grumbled. He found a note stuck to the bottom of the coffee machine and shrugged. He was more interested in what was in the tray. It had a glass of water, cutlery, a cupcake, and a covered plate. He blinked back tears when he opened the plate and saw the pie.

He was so hungry he guzzled the food in a rush. And desiring to be in her good books, he washed his plates even though he hated wetting his hands. He chuckled when he realised the note was from

Stella. He smiled sheepishly. He didn't need to find an excuse, he had been offered one.

Four days would be enough time to get Kelechi on board, he thought. He hoped.

Kelechi was not one to leave the door unlocked when she was naked, more so after living with intrusive in-laws. She had thought long and hard and knew she had one thing to do – have a child of her own and leave him to his new wife. Therefore, she would have to let her guard down, swallow her pride, and let her husband in. She had to woo him; discarding the towel, she tiptoed back to the bathroom without the towel, feeling lightheaded from trepidation and desire. The sudden shake of her head caused her to slip, knocking down the flower vases she'd planned to take to the kitchen.

Johnson heard the breaking-and-crashing and broke into the bathroom.

Startled, she yelped and steadied herself when she saw that it was her husband.

He swept the shards of glass to the side with his flip-flops then stretched his hand towards her, but she brushed his hands away and staggered. He caught Kelechi by the hand and slung her over his shoulder before carrying her out of the bathroom. As soon as he set her down, she made an attempt to leave the bed, but he pulled her back and made to go.

Kelechi shivered.

Thinking she was cold, he picked the towel up, wrapped it around her, and simultaneously dried her.

Kelechi closed her legs when he tried to clean between her thighs. Johnson nudged, but she didn't budge. He picked up her cream and offered it to her, and she turned away from him, creating a gap between them. Her ribcage trapped the speed of her heartbeat.

Seeing her naked for the first time since they'd known each other caused him good grief, so while she massaged the cream onto her body, he undressed.

She handed him the cream, slanted her head, and smiled. She may not have planned it this way, but an opportunity was an opportunity. Anxious and excited, she gritted her teeth as he lathered her skin with the cream. The trepidation of the impending pain that came with making love for the first time threatened to overwhelm her. Still, his hands on her skin tormented her with various sensations and, at varying degrees, which she found breathtakingly strange and curious. As he wrapped his arms around her, her anxieties dwindled. Her heart raced further as he snuggled and kissed her. She let out an involuntary sigh as he began to knead her breast. Moaning, she arched her back eagerly with an increasing desire for more.

She felt Johnson shudder as she writhed in his arms, his manhood throbbing on her buttocks. She bit her lips when he slid a hand down her midriff and purred, parting her legs to welcome him. Her mind protested, her body yearned, but it was hard to think through anything, much less decide. Mesmerised by the new sensations blossoming in her, she called him every fond name she could think of, and subsequently groaned her protest when he abruptly stopped.

Johnson brushed the clothes off the bed. Desperate for union, he carried her to it.

Kelechi's response to his forceful thrust was a piercing scream.

Johnson froze, shocked that she was still a virgin. He wrapped his arms around her, cooing, kissing, and caressing her when she tried to push him off her until she was urging him again and didn't stop until they were spent.

He caught Kelechi as she tried to shy away from him and wrapped his arms around her. He wiped away the tears that streamed down her eyes then made a personal promise to make up for his wrong doings.

As he stroked her face, he sighed. His anguish at the time he married Stella, was his inability to share the pain of Kelechi cheating on him. Now his anguish was born from the fact that he didn't trust her enough to wait for him. Restlessly he pondered, wondering why he never gave his parents' words a second thought, especially after the stunt they'd pulled before he left Nigeria.

He didn't believe Maurice, but he'd always trusted his parents.

"I love you. I never stopped loving you."

He smiled, glad that he finally dared to tell her how he felt about her after all these years. He yawned as he pulled the duvet over them, only noticing then that it had no covering just before his eyelids closed.

Kelechi heard him say something about love as she dozed off.

CHAPTER 5

The doorbell chimed. It was quite early, but Kelechi welcomed the distraction. The past days with Stella away had been filled with herself and Johnson ruffling the bed. They barely left the bed except for essential needs, to use the toilet or eat. Hearing the chime, a second time, she frowned and looked at the time. Johnson had left for work, so she assumed it was the mailman and opened the door without checking.

Kelechi blinked when her eyes fell on the unfamiliar faces that flanked her friend; they reminded her of sandwich and the fact that she had not had breakfast. She tried to stifle the chuckle that was bubbling up and sighed dramatically.

"Simi, how *nawh*? Come in," Kelechi reluctantly stepped aside to let Simisola and the other women into the house she wasn't ready to call home.

Although she was glad to have company, she was uncomfortable with the new two. More so, she'd assumed that it was too early to be entertaining guests. But when they mumbled their greetings and brushed past her, she couldn't decide between amusement and annoyance.

She offered them cake and wine. When they made weird faces, she smiled, admit it was an unusual combination.

"Simi," Kelechi nudged her friend. "You didn't introduce me to your *friends*."

"Ha! True talk." Simisola agreed, cleared her throat, and poked the fair lady beside her. The lady could somewhat be mistaken for Kelechi, except for her stronger features, huge breasts, and very fair skin. "Zainab, meet my friend, Kelechi. We went to Riv-Poly together. Without her, I for no graduate. Zainab and I are neighbours, and our kids go to the same school." "So, we're not friends then," Zainab murmured, pouting.

Kelechi frowned, amused.

"Sorry," Simisola said with a wave of her hand then pointed at her other friend. "That's Motiráyò. I met my ex-husband through her. We met when I started top-up."

Kelechi's frown deepened. "Ex-husband? When?"

"Don't mind her o!" Motiráyò said, smiling. "Just call me Áyò,".

"Zainab, Áyò," Kelechi nodded at each other. Áyò was buxom as she was tall, taller than Simisola, and less a few inches to Kelechi.

"Top-up?" Kelechi asked.

"Yes, to change my HND to a degree," Áyò murmured and raised a meaning brow at Simisola.

"Oh!" Kelechi mumbled with a nod. *A great idea! Another thing to explore.*

As Simisola and the new two started talking about their kids and showing off pictures, Kelechi got lost in her grieve. Impatiently, she waited for them to leave as she suspected they did it to spite her.

Two hours later, she began to wonder how long a guest was supposed to stay before it became impolite. Four hours later, they were hungry. She decided to feed them with the food they'd brought. So they wouldn't feel slighted, she brought it in two large plates and made the excuse of having no more plates. She already felt insulted that they'd made the *eba* themselves and took their advice with feigned gratitude.

Also, she hoped they'd leave before her husband returned. If there was one thing Johnson hated, it was the invasion of his privacy. She, however, detested it. She didn't see them leaving anytime soon, so she looked at the time right after they had eaten and gasped and gave them her best surprised look then made an excuse of having somewhere to be. She was suspiciously surprised when they all wanted to stay, insisting on waiting to greet her husband. She decided to tell them to leave bluntly, but Simisola beat her to it.

"Will you be attending mass this weekend?" Simisola asked as she walked them down the stairs.

"Of course!" Kelechi quickly replied.

"I'll pick you up Sunday, eh!" Simisola said eagerly.

Kelechi pretended not to hear her.

"Which parish?" Áyò asked.

"Na church dem dey go!" Zainab retorted.

"I know." Áyò snapped, stung.

Zainab pulled back and thinned her lips, staring gloomily at the other women.

Kelechi reluctantly walked them to Simisola's car and waved them goodbye. She was so relieved to discharge them that she'd forgotten she was pretending to go out. Deciding to take a walk, she turned to Gaskarth Road and then to Millfield Road and got lost. She walked from one end to another on Millfield Road twice, trying to figure out where she'd missed her way. By the third time, she saw a bereft road sign named Playfield Road. It was a familiar name. Then she remembered that it started at Watling Avenue; somewhat relieved, she decided to walk to the other end of it. It was not until she got to St Alphage that she noticed she was heading in the wrong direction; so that by the time she got home, her feet were numb.

"Where were you?" Johnson asked angrily, standing on the gangway of the neighbouring compound.

Infuriated, Kelechi hissed and walked around him, not stopping.

"Why didn't you carry your phone with you?" he asked, digging into his pocket for his keys.

Kelechi gritted her teeth; She had forgotten to leave with her phone, and he was the third person to tell her that in the same week.

"I was worried about you," Johnson murmured, his tone now heavy with concern.

She waited for him to open the door and pushed past him when he wouldn't get out of the way.

"I'm sorry about earlier," he said and grabbed her hand.

She had hoped to see remorse from him, something to show that he was sorry for what he had put her through, for marrying someone else. She had resisted the urge to ask him, plead with him. Annoyed that she still longed for him amidst her pain, she pulled her hand back so forcefully she hit her nose. She bent down to nurse her nose and tried to nurse her feet at the same time. Johnson pulled her with him into the sitting room then gently nudged her into the settee.

"I'll be right back," he mumbled as he went into

the bathroom.

Soon after he left, their phones rang.

Kelechi peered at the screen of Johnson's phone and angrily switched it off, muttering, "I'll try to tolerate sharing my husband with you, but that is as far as it goes." Then frowning at the unusual number on the screen, she hesitantly picked hers.

"Hello?"

"Hi, its Zainab," a small voice said.

"Zainab? How did you get my number?"

"I think from Simisola. I just wanted to ask you when it would be best to get the bowls. Sorry, they're a family heirloom," Zainab said quickly.

"Oh, it's okay," Kelechi said and paused for a while. "I'll let you know. Thank you for the food."

Johnson walked in with a towel wrapped around his waist. "I was thinking of placing an order. What would you like to eat?"

She shrugged as she roused herself, murmuring, "Excuse me." As soon as she entered the kitchen, she emptied the leftover of Áyò and Zainab's food in the bin, spritzed the kitchen to disguise their smell, and walked into her husband as she made to leave.

"Why did you switch off my phone?" Johnson asked with a dubious smile.

"Do you receive calls from work at this time?" she asked matter-of-factly.

"No?" he answered with a frown, a little hesitantly.

"Then it shouldn't be on."

He chuckled. "You know you didn't turn it off because of work."

"Really?" she asked, staring coldly at him.

The look in her eyes muted his next statement. He stepped out of the way for her to pass, and then he slapped her buttocks.

"Don't do that again," she warned, waving a solitary finger at him. "Dry those clothes and put the next batch in."

By the time Kelechi came out of the bathroom, Johnson had dished out the food he'd ordered, set up Netflix on the TV, and whisked out a new throw in her favourite colour: grey.

She entered the sitting room. It was warm, the light had been toned down, and a bottle of wine lay in an ice bucket she hadn't seen before. She picked up the note left to Johnson by his landlord, instructing him to get rid of the things in the shed and made a mental note to take a look at it the following day.

"How did work go?" she asked as she made her way to the settee.

He looked up to see her in a silver satin side-tie chemise and gulped. He cleared his throat, his voice now husky as he described his day.

Her grandmother had always said: 'let a man

see enough to desire more.' She tucked her feet between his and pulled the throw over them before handing him his plate of food. He'd already poured the champagne. She smiled inwardly, acknowledging the fact he still had a soft spot for her. Determined to take advantage of it, she listened to every word that came out of his mouth, knowing how he loved the attention.

She eyed the frosting glass and grimaced, unsure of the effect the bubbly liquid would have on her. She hesitantly picked her glass and sipped it; the taste reminded her of heavily diluted lime juice.

They watched her favourite, *Only Fools and Horses*. Johnson watched her laugh; he missed hearing her laughter. Smiling, he wondered what else he'd forgotten about her and pulled her closer to him and lost his balance.

In adjusting her weight to lean on him, she accidentally brushed his manhood, and his reaction to her touch made her tingle with excitement.

Johnson pulled her to himself and began to tickle her until she could no longer take it, then gazed adoringly at her. With a mischievous smile, he slung her over his shoulder and walked briskly to the bedroom.

CHAPTER 6

Kelechi woke up as soon as it was morning. Overcome with embarrassment at how easily she'd given herself to her husband. Again. Desperate to be out of sight when he woke, she slowly pulled off her side of the duvet and withdrew from him.

Johnson caught her hand, pulled her back to bed, and began to kiss her. And all her inhibitions were instantly forgotten. He was so gentle she couldn't hold back tears, and a tiny part of her mind hoped that their union had a chance, what with another woman in the picture.

She woke up a few hours later to the smell of coffee, eggs, toast, and bacon. She saw the tray on the side of the bed he'd slept in and giggled. He had made her breakfast. Hungry, she looked up at him, smiling shyly. It was the first time she'd seem him stark naked. It was distracting enough for her to avert her eyes with her hair.

She felt a little awkward with his watching her eat, only distracted temporarily by the doorbell.

Suspecting that it was Stella, she gritted her

teeth and balled her fists.

He peered through a crack in the curtain. Unable to make out their guests were, he went to the door to inspect, returned a few seconds later, and whispered, "Your friend - the one that picked up the cake - is here with other friends."

"Oh," surprised, relieved, then alarmed, she asked in a loud whisper, "did you let them in?"

Johnson shook his head.

She stretched her hand to get her phone and turned it off.

"Do I open the door for them?" Johnson asked hesitantly.

"Did I invite them?" she hissed and put her hair up in a bun.

Chuckling, Johnson raised his hands in surrender then tucked his hands in his pocket. His eyes dilated at the movement of her breasts. He took quick and long strides to the bed. In one swift move, decked the tray onto the chest of drawers, tossed the duvet aside, and nudged her back as he kissed her.

Unknown to the couple, Simisola and her counterparts watched them through the side of the window that the curtain had still not obscured.

Kelechi woke up hours later. *Lovemaking is indeed a delicious feat; one I'm not ready to give up*, she acknowledged and stretched. Once she noticed that she was alone, she began to grumble. Annoyed that he may have gone to Stella's side, she strode into the sitting room nude.

The instant she entered the sitting room, Johnson tucked a piece of paper under him. She'd noticed that he was a little distracted earlier, but now that he hid the letter on seeing her, she knew something was wrong. Not knowing how to broach the subject, she decided not to ask; she could always snoop when he wasn't watching. Perhaps being innocuous was the way to go for now. As a duty, she had to acquaint herself with anything linked with her husband. She sauntered toward him with feigned timidity.

Johnson stretched his hand toward her, and she took it, and as he kissed her, she smiled satisfied that at this rate, she'll be pregnant.

Sated, he pulled her close and began to massage her back.

"Are you ovulating?" he asked, deliberately slow.

She stiffened and raised a suspicious brow as she stammered, "I don't know."

"How can you not know when you're ovulating?" Johnson shrieked, shifting from her.

Miffed by his sudden coldness, she shrugged. "I didn't know I needed to."

"I'll teach you how to check. What was the last

day of your last period?"

"The day I came," she lied and adjusted herself to distract him.

Johnson calculated then exhaled deeply, relieved that he would be ready for any further complication. He was equally glad to have cared for her enough to touch her and discover the truth. There was something primal about being the first to unwrap such purity, something manly, the significance of unblemished completion. But his happiness was tinged with worry as he lay by her. He mulled over what their relationship would be like when Stella finally returned.

"When is she coming back?" Kelechi asked as if she'd read his mind. She knew Stella was supposed to have returned that morning.

He stiffened. "Next weekend."

"Mmm," she readjusted her weight.

"What?"

"Nothing," she said with a shrug. She was already thinking of what she would be doing when Stella returned. She'd been thinking of if from the day she entered the flat.

"Come on," he nudged her. "Tell me."

"It seems you don't want me to bear your children," she deflected.

He lifted her face. "How can you say that?"

Kelechi closed her eyes, slanting her head and murmured through clenched teeth. "Because of

Stella."

"You know that's not true."

Kelechi sniggered, rolling her eyes.

"Don't be like this!"

"Like what?" she turned away from him. She looked at his arms around her waist, and tears streamed down her face. "How would you feel if I was with another man?"

"But you weren't."

"Because I promised."

"Is this fight because I want us to hold off on having babies?"

She finally untangled herself.

He blocked her path. Chuckling, he mumbled, "you weren't this angry when we made out. You weren't angry at all."

Stung, she retaliated by shoving him as she made a swift exit. She'd shoved him so hard that he hit the back of his head on the doorpost

Johnson scrambled to get to her, but she had locked the door.

Kelechi slunk to the ground, sobbing and brooding. *What can I do now? Even if I was to walk out of this marriage, what will I say I've benefited from it? I don't have a job, money to rent a place, or transport to go back home.* She cried because she knew her only option was to swallow her pride and stay until she could get on her feet.

"Nwunye'm," Johnson kept calling from the other side of the door.

She knew he was leaning on the door because the hinge creaked. She felt the pain in her chest again, and she folded her legs, wrapped her arms around them, trying to hide from the pain.

She loved him. She saved all she had to be with him. Now, she was afraid to think of what the future might hold. She'd heard of men marrying women to get their papers; she never believed her husband would be one of them.

"I'm sorry, please open the door," Johnson pleaded.

She ignored him for almost an hour, but her bladder was burning with urgency, so she unlocked the door and quickly brushed past him.

Johnson went into the bedroom to wait for her, but she headed for the kitchen when she came out. She warmed three of the cupcakes and made a promise not to bake more. Distractedly, she began to pace and then started to prepare another dough. Realising too late, she decided to make another batch of cake. While she waited for the cake to finish baking, she began to clean the sitting room, forgetting that she wanted to leave it for Stella to do.

She hadn't called home since she arrived two weeks ago. The plan had been to call as soon as she found Johnson. Now it didn't seem to matter.

Nothing did.

She returned to the kitchen and began to wash, slowly at first, then more forcefully until her hands were raw, pale, and wrinkly. Sighing, she kicked the vacuum cleaner to the sitting room to finish what she'd started.

Johnson angrily stalked into the sitting room a few hours later, waving his phone at her.

"Where have you been?" he asked as he tucked his phone into his pocket.

Kelechi didn't answer him; she moved the new colour-coded heap of clothes out of the way to continue vacuuming.

"Are you not the one I'm talking to?" he asked, his tone demeaning.

Kelechi pursed her lips, turned off the vacuum cleaner, picked up one set of clothes, and turned in the direction of the kitchen.

"Kelechi," Johnson snapped, blocking her path again. "I asked you a question."

Kelechi looked at him inquisitively.

"Where have you been? Why didn't you tell my parents you were travelling? Which man did you leave with?"

Kelechi sized him up and manoeuvred around him and went into the kitchen. As she bent down to tuck the clothes into the machine, her husband pulled her up by the hand.

She screamed in frustration and asked. "What

is it? What right do you have to question me?"

"The right of a husband," he muttered as he moved closer and accidentally knocked down some plates from the rack.

She picked up the broom and a dustpan beside her and handed it to him. He bent down to sweep it and gave them to her. "Answer me, Kelechi."

"What was the question?" she asked as she emptied the dustpan.

He repeated it.

"I have been at my cousin's. I came into the country with him. He gave me a phone and your address just before..." Kelechi brushed past her husband as she left the kitchen then turned to face him squarely.

"I'm their daughter-in-law and nothing else," she spat, then picked up a discarded book and frowned at it before shoving it at him.

He took the book, glanced over it, and tossed it on the table. "You could have told me. They've been worried."

"Worried? Really?" She mocked and let out a long hiss.

"You didn't tell anyone you were leaving for three weeks. What if something had happened to you? What if you didn't find me?"

"All these questions," Kelechi chuckled detestably as she gestured. "Are they because I've turned your house into our home? Or because you're now open to a little discomfort."

"Meaning?"

"Meaning? Meaning that you would pretend I am your sister when she returns. And that places you in a precarious position," she sniggered defiantly then looked at his arms around her for a while, then struggled to break free from his embrace.

Defeated, he let her go and softly added. "It's only for a time."

She chuckled again, tears streaming down her face. "How dare you? How dare you stand there and defend your actions? You think I'm you, that couldn't respect the anticity of his vows?"

"Kelechi, watch your mouth!"

She raised her head defiantly. "Or what? You've been perusing another woman's privates for how long now? So, what have you been doing with her? Did she wait until you were married? Is she the only person you've cheated on me with? Have you had any infection since you started having sexual intercourse?" She stopped as she tried to control her involuntary quake.

"Kelechi," he exclaimed, staring at her, aghast.

"Oh, please!" she waved nonchalantly. "If you want someone to order around, go to Stella."

"Enough!"

She shuddered mockingly and returned to vacuuming.

Johnson's phone started ringing again. He looked at the screen and frowned. Worried that she'd raise her voice while he spoke to his boss, he walked out of the sitting room.

She watched him leave and clucked her tongue, then remembered the promises she'd made to him. Determined not to make his mistakes, she decided that no matter how angry she was at him, she would cook for him and not deprive him of sharing her bed. With that, she went to the kitchen to look for what to cook.

Johnson returned a while later, fully dressed. "Nwunye'm?"

Kelechi sighed heavily and reluctantly mumbled. "Yes?" She spun, gritting her teeth to prevent words slipping out of her mouth and grimaced. He was a handsome man, more so with his glasses on. She would have given him a compliment if he'd apologized. Yet she couldn't help adjusting the collar of his polo shirt.

"I'm off to work. I'm needed, urgently."

"I didn't know you had a job."

"I've been working for years now. I thought you knew."

"When was the last time you wrote to or called your wife?"

Johnson gestured about to explain but stopped himself when he saw her back turned to him. He sighed and left at the same time.

“We’re out of foodstuff o!” she called after him and hissed.

“I’ll be back in a few hours.”

She clucked her tongue and turned off the offending vacuum cleaner.

CHAPTER 7

Restless after cleaning, she took a long bath and paced. She had outdone herself; there was nothing left to clean or cook or bake. Having nowhere to go, she wore a maroon-coloured shorts with a white tank top and lay in bed.

Bored and tired of waiting for him to come to her, she went to the sitting room. Johnson's head was buried in his drawings since he returned. He'd been at it all day. She turned off the lights to distract him and turned the standing lamp on a few seconds later and began a striptease.

Johnson blinked, several times with a weird smile on his face. He watched eagerly, swallowed, and became a tad impatient as he felt she was too slow. As she wriggled and wiggled, he shuddered at his fantasy come true. As she inched closer, he began to undress. He was going to make this a night to remember, he thought as he licked his lips, welcoming her effrontery.

Kelechi woke up and went to ease herself and returned to the clang of stilettos. Suspecting it could be Stella, she rushed into the room and picked up her husband's phone from the bedside chest and made her way to the front door. She stealthily bolted it then tiptoed back to the bedroom after switching off her husband's phone. Stella pressed the bell and banged the door, but Kelechi ignored her. It was even harder when Stella started banging on the bedroom window because Johnson, like herself, was a light sleeper. The noise ended with a click of the letterbox.

Fortunately, the sound didn't wake him. It, however, kept Kelechi awake. Unable to go back to sleep, she put her time into preparing what they'd wear to Mass. She read Stella's message and sniggered. It read:

> *I will be back between 9am and 10am this morning. Switch your phone on, and don't lock me out again.*

It was almost morning before she got to bed. Bent on giving her husband pleasant memories of their time together she parted his legs submitted to his pleasing her. She hoped it was only a matter of time before he accepted that they couldn't keep up the charade.

CHAPTER 8

But they did. Kelechi's desires outweighed her need to divulge Johnson's secret. Besides, Stella was a constant irritant, always stroking her husband. It had been two weeks since she'd been alone with her husband.

The house was quiet except for the sporadic calls Stella received. She wished the woman had gone to work. For some reason, Stella was home any day Johnson was.

Something had happened, something he was keeping to himself. He was usually detached, but she could always bring him out of that reverie. It wouldn't have bothered her, perhaps a little, but her concern was for her husband's sudden change, and because Stella was in the house, she couldn't inspect it.

In a way, she was pleased that he wasn't always making love to Stella; she wasn't sure she could cope if he did.

Kelechi sniggered. Stella was a lot like Johnson. She had begun to notice too many similarities between them that she began to worry.

*

Stella excitedly barged in without knocking and said in a shrill voice. “Oh, Chi, thank you so much.”

“For what?” Kelechi asked, irritated that Stella had distracted her, especially as she’d expected it to be her husband.

“My silk dress! You found it!” Stella retorted, stretching the hand with a red dress draped over it. “I’ve been looking for it forever.”

“Be tidy, and it wouldn’t be so hard,” Kelechi spat.

Stella bowled over and looked around. She pointed at herself as if asking an internal question. Tongue in cheek, fuming, she withdrew, briskly walked into the sitting room. “Did you hear that? Or did I imagine it?”

“Imagine what?” Johnson asked, feigning ignorance as he continued typing away on his laptop.

“I’m talking to you, Johnson!”

“What is it Stella?” Johnson sighed exasperated, annoyed that she forcefully shut his laptop.

“Did you not hear how she spoke to me?” Stella asked, her voice sharp.

“How did she speak to you?” he asked,

unconcerned.

"What's going on? What's your relationship with her?"

He set the laptop aside and crossed his arms. "What do you think?"

"What!? Is that all you've got to say?" She furiously asked, arms flailing as she glared at him. "Are you fucking her?"

Johnson sighed, relieved that she was only suspicious, worn because of the hide and seek game. It felt strange that he'd obsess about both women simultaneously so much so he was considering a threesome.

"What?" Stella asked, looking confused.

He muttered under his breath.

"What?"

"I said, 'only a man holding a machete fears that another may do the same'."

"What's that supposed to mean?"

Johnson got up, pulling on a shirt. "If you weren't cheating on me, you wouldn't suspect me of cheating on you." He looked coolly at her, and for a split second, his fears were confirmed. Shaken, he walked away.

Stella watched him leave the sitting room and grimaced before quickly joining him in the toilet. "I'm sorry. I suspected you. I know you're not. It's just that, well, you've been busy and distracted. She was so mean to me. and you said nothing, and you refuse to tell me your relationship with that girl."

He sighed. He knew what she would want next. He was worried that Kelechi would hear them. Instead, Stella waited for him to flush the toilet and then sat on the lid. As she put her mouth on his manhood, he closed his eyes and imagined it was Kelechi.

Kelechi woke up to cheerful sounds coming from the sitting room. Stella was giggling at something their husband had murmured. It annoyed her so much that she chose to leave the house than remain cooped up in the room. She hadn't opened the window for a week.

Deciding it was time to stop wallowing in self-pity, she opened it right after taking her bath. As she left the room, she glanced back, wondering if she should tell Johnson that she was heading out, but Stella's giggles stopped her.

She gritted her teeth when she got to the door but stayed behind. What was she going to see if she went into the sitting room? While trying to calm her nerves, she twisted her mouth and unhooked a coat, and her eyes fell on her husband's bomber jacket. Unabashed, she rummaged the pockets, found his key and wallet and sighed with relief.

She opened the wallet and found four bankcards, one was not in his name, and neither was it in Stella's name. She shrugged and replaced them, taking all the cash she'd found. She hadn't bothered to cook for him since Stella's return, mainly because he didn't acknowledge her. She was equally tired of bingeing on the madeira and sponge cakes she'd safely tucked away.

If she hadn't dragged her husband to the movies after Mass that Sunday, they wouldn't have gone out together. Tired of waiting for an opportunity to be alone with her husband, she hoped she could create one by giving him a home-cooked meal. After all, food was a way to a man's heart, abi?

Unsure of which dish to make, she bought too many things and now needed help with carrying them. The man who insisted she should get more malt drinks and paid for it decided to walk her home. Torn between disposing of him and getting him to help her, she let one of the boys from the shop help her take her things. The shop owner was more than willing to help because she looked distressed. She stumbled into the house after untangling the key from her earpiece. She pushed everything in with her feet as she tried to close to the door.

Bopping her head to the music, she took off her jacket then danced with two bags in her hand as she made her way to the kitchen and froze. Johnson's head was on the floor with Stella on him at the edge of the chair.

Knowing that Stella was about to orgasm, she yelped. Johnson pushed Stella off him and tried to shield himself with a pillow. Kelechi mumbled an apology and walked into the kitchen with a satisfied smile. Though his reaction made her sigh with relief, his words haunted her.

'Be less conservative, more flexible', he'd said. She had to learn to please him in bed as Stella did. But was it worth it? Would that make him hers? She'd tried, but was it enough?

Stella groaned and stamped her feet in frustration. "I'm moving back to the room right now!"

Johnson, wearing a frown, pulled up his jogging bottoms.

He mumbled to hide his embarrassment. "We agreed to this, did we not?"

"So how do we have sex with freedom when, where, and how we want?" Stella asked, still irked.

"Stella," he stretched his hand to pull her close, but she stepped away, shaking her head and weaving a solitary finger at him.

"Urgh! I don't mind being seen fucking. You do." She said pointedly and began cussing. "Come on, Stella..."

She waved her hands. "Argh! Do something

about this!" With that, she walked away.

"We're supposed to be at Cherub's party." He didn't want to attend it because he didn't know anyone in her new IT crowd. He just didn't want her to keep prodding him.

"Oh dear! I forgot!" She quickly ran the bath and returned to take his hand. He shook his head but joined her. As they had their shower, she tried to prime him to no avail. She suspected it was because he didn't want to attend the party.

Johnson couldn't forget the scorn in Kelechi's eyes. He was doing things he was supposed to do to her with another woman. What woman would cope with that? He could imagine her torture. But he'd come too far to abandon this project now.

Johnson quickly got dressed so he could have an opportunity to speak with Kelechi before they left. Perhaps Stella suspected because she kept calling his attention to something while she got dressed. The doorbell chimed, and he quickly went to answer it.

"Hello, you must be Mr Thomas."

He raised a brow at the woman whose hair glistening like liquid gold under the porch light.

"I'll like to speak to your wife," the woman continued.

"Who is it?" Stella asked, still running back and forth between the bathroom and the sitting room.

"Stella," the lady muttered in a steely voice.

Stella thinned her lips and rested a hand on her waist. "Otis."

"It's Megan to you."

Johnson held his breath and slowly released it. He'd heard a lot about the woman.

"Urgh! What do you want?" Stella asked impatiently.

Megan gestured. "May I come in?"

"No, you may not. What do you want?" Stella asked as she stepped forward, forming a wedge between Johnson and Megan.

"My husband needs you to take care of something."

"What?" Stella snapped, quite irritated.

"You're his employee. He is your boss. Find out!" Megan baited then gave Johnson a curt nod and walked away.

Amused, Johnson glanced at Stella.

"It's not funny," she scolded then groaned. "I hate my job."

"No, you don't."

"No, I don't," she agreed, wrapped her arms around his waist and looked up at him. "I'm sorry."

He nodded.

"Hey! Why don't you go to the party? I'll join you as soon as I'm done."

He groaned.

"Shy guy," she murmured, shaking her head.

“People pleaser,” he retorted and slapped her buttocks. When she giggled, he grimaced, remembering Kelechi’s response to the same action.

As she unhooked her coat, she asked. “How do I look?”

“Great.”

She still looked into the mirror before shutting the door.

He hated it when she did that. “Why ask for one’s opinion if you don’t need it?” he muttered and locked it.

“Is she gone?” Kelechi asked in a condescending tone.

Johnson jumped, knocking one foot on the other. He turned to see her leaning on the doorpost and limped towards her.

“Brunch will be ready in ten minutes,” she said and walked back into the bedroom, locking the door behind her.

Curiously, he went to the kitchen and saw the soup she’d made him. Her compassion stirred his heart and closed his eyes, pained. She had cooked his favourite: *native soup*, amongst other things. Sighing, he thought. *She must have used up the money in my wallet - these women. You two are high maintenance.*

To even her effort, he decided to make *fufu*.

They ate silently and watched a movie. She

asked him how to use Netflix. Johnson, loving the platform, introduced other ideas. Half-listening, she pondered on whom his heart lay with: did he loved her as much as he did Stella. He and Stella fought all the time, and she had a feeling that they had sex right after, just like they'd done earlier.

She didn't know how long she would cope with having to share him because hearing them was difficult. But seeing them tore her insides apart.

CHAPTER 9

Johnson removed the plate from her hand and dipped her other hand in the bowl of tepid water. He squeezed her freed hand as he washed the other then pulled her into his arms, soothing her as she sobbed. There were things that words couldn't rectify, and if there was, he didn't know. He shuddered as he remembered her question – '*how would you feel if I was with another man?*

He closed his eyes to hold back tears. Even with the tension, what he wanted to do was rip her clothes apart and devour her right there. He grimaced; it was an awful thing to think of at a time like this, but his manhood didn't think so.

He let out an exasperated sigh. Admittedly, Kelechi was his weakness; ever since he saw her backside all those years ago. It was hard for him to resist her when he saw her bent over firewood. He cleared his throat and clenched his teeth as the tension in his groin increased. She was his weakness, indeed. At the time he'd met her marriage was not in the cards. It was supposed to be a fling.

It was season of Advent. Christmas songs could be heard in many households and on children's lips. That humble day was a Saturday in 2007; his university had been on strike for months. His cousin was coming back from the US. If you forgot, his mother would remind you that without her, his cousin wouldn't have been a graduate, but all she did was pay for his flight ticket. His cousin had earned himself a scholarship.

His mother had a gathering of sorts. He wanted to leave the house, hating crowd and the noise that came with them. This Saturday was different. People piled into the compound like ants on a cube of sugar. It was a humdrum of busy bees. Some clusters butchered yam, onions; another made a tremendous effort of panel-beating palm fruits, ogbono seed. Close to the kitchen door, a younger group of women were huddled over cassava and corn.

Their activities did nothing to dispel his boredom. He didn't even want company, especially his cousins, and they were all over the place. Even his room was fast becoming a pedestrian walkway.

In front of the house beside the udala tree were litters of women around various pots in varied stages of cooking. This was his mother's setting.

He'd looked hungrily at the portable radio.

The kiosks had been out of battery for days. He had used up any energy it had left after placing them under the sun. With the fuel scarcity, the generator only came on at night. An opportunity arose when his mother went around the back. He quickly tucked his feet in his plimsolls. He tiptoed until he got to the front door and almost ran to the gate.

"Thomas! Come, come, come, just the person I was looking for."

His shoulder fell on hearing his mother's voice, defeated he turned to face her.

"You were supposed to be helping out. At least, supervising those good for nothing boys. I hope they roast the goats well. I don't trust any of them with my money. You need to have seen the skinniness of the goats they bought for me. I don't trust any of them with money. Now that you're here, you might as well make yourself useful." She tugged his arm to pull him closer, and then she undid one end of her wrapper. He looked at the crumpled naira notes and felt pity for them. "Here, take, go and buy me firewood."

He reluctantly stretched his hand to her and muttered under his breath. "So much for a quick exit."

But his mother had heard. "Your cousins have been busy all morning while you've been galivanting. Oya go and buy me firewood," she hissed and readjusted her wrapper. "Imagine, the insolence!"

Johnson watched her walk away and looked down at the money then shook his head. He didn't know where to get firewood or the price. Defeated, he went to the kiosk to ask Bassey, its owner, and his friend.

Ogbogo, another friend, a welder, was there instead.

"Ogbogo! I greet o!" He'd said cheerily as he climbed the little porch and sat on the bench Ogbogo had just vacated to attend to a customer and waited.

"Morning my brother. How far nah?"

"I suppose dey ask you. Wetin you dey do for here?"

"My guy," Ogbogo retorted and joined him on the bench. "Bassey go collect im goods. I just tanda dey wait am. How far nah?"

Johnson grimaced ruefully. "Firewood o!"

Ogbogo stared at his friend, amused.

"Momsie send me message. Abeg, where I fit buy firewood?"

Ogbogo thought briefly and shook his head. "I no sure, you know sey today na Saturday."

Just then, an okada rider came to a halt beside them. Behind him were bales of toiletries and whatnots. It moved just as Ogbogo went towards it. A head appeared, and Johnson smiled, shaking his head. It was Bassey. He joined Ogbogo in assisting Bassey with his ware.

"Bassey, as you don return make I begin waka." Ogbogo jangled his keys and walked to the motorcycle leaning against the wall near the kiosk. Then he brought it around the front of the kiosk and shook it to gauge the amount of fuel he had. "That your Calabar girlfriend carry yam comot o!"

"You no sell anything?"

"Sell wetin? I just tell you say your Calabar girlfriend carry yam comot." Ogbogo turned to Johnson and asked. "Water dey my mouth as I talk am?"

Amused, Johnson shook his head.

Bassey looked unhappy as he scratched his shaven head and sighed heavily. "Na wa o!"

Ogbogo poked Johnson and pointed at Bassey. "You dey see this guy? Na my church mind I take 'ep am o!"

Johnson massaged his arm. "Ogbogo, e don do." As much as he enjoyed a difference in the activity, he didn't want it to get out of hand. He stretched his hand towards Bassey. "Bassey, how you dey?"

Bassey sighed again as they shook hands. "Bros, I dey o!"

Ogbogo hissed and made a show of getting on top of his motorbike. "I dey go my shed."

"Ogbogo, wait nah! Make I give you one shot." Bassey turned to the counter behind him.

Ogbogo feigned reluctance.

"As a big boy," Johnson nudged.

Ogbogo let out an inflated sigh, parked his bike, and joined them on the small bench.

"Which one?" Bassey asked, pulling out a drawer with varied blends of local whisky.

"Ogogoro," Ogbogo answered, quite eagerly.

"Thomas, which one?"

"Dogonyaro." Johnson muttered gingerly.

"Hiah! You get malaria?" Ogbogo asked, looking concerned.

Johnson shook his head. "Ehen, Bassey where I fit buy firewood."

"Na Kelechi nah. I hear sey her firewood make sense."

"Where I go fit find this Kelechi?"

Bassey pondered and clicked his finger. "I no know o! I know sey you fit find am for the other end, after that Cherubim Church. Ogbogo, you suppose know the place nah!"

"Which place?" Ogbogo swatted a fly and stared at his friends.

"The Kelechi girl you suppose know am," Johnson said, a little impatiently.

"Who be Kelechi?" Ogbogo asked just before downing the last of his ogogoro.

Bassey hissed and shook his head before

clicking his finger. "You sabi that girl wen beat Jesus-Brother for market?"

Ogbogo laughed, nodding. "Okay, na that side I dey go sef." He patted his papa's cap, rousing. "Oya, make we waka."

They rode on Ogbogo's bike for about ten minutes. Ogbogo distracted him with the events that had taken place in the village while he was away. When they got to the crossroads, Ogbogo pointed him in the direction of Kelechi's house. He had been meaning to ask about the girl who fought in the market and why but didn't get a chance to as Ogbogo had turned his bike in the opposite direction, heading to his welding shop.

When Johnson got to the address, he found the gate open. He knocked. No one answered. After a second try, he decided to go inside. As he wasn't sure of Kelechi's age, he shouted, "pesin dey this house?"

"Anyone here?" he asked as he went to the left side of the compound. He stumbled to a halt when he saw a woman's behind. She was bent over a few firewood beside a mountain of them.

"Excuse me!" he stammered.

Kelechi straightened, one of the timbers in her hand.

Johnson raised his hands in surrender. "I come in peace."

"I thought you were..." she lowered her hand

but didn't drop the wood. "How may I help you?"

Unsure, he asked. "Kelechi?"

"Ehen," she looked him over suspiciously. "Who is asking?"

Johnson was flabbergasted. Here he was thinking Kelechi was a hairy giant. He swallowed his words. What stood in front of him was a girl that was a few inches shorter than him, a gap-toothed beauty. He squinted at the flimsy dress that clung to her curves. Do you wear this out of this compound? He asked in his thought. He was human, and Jesus-Brother was not insane to want to take advantage of this woman, he was just out of control, just like he was feeling at the moment.

"Oga!" Kelechi called out impatiently.

"Eh...!?"

Kelechi raised a brow at him; her arms crossed, causing her breast to jut up.

He groaned, trying not to yelp in excitement. His heart raced. He frowned, feeling somewhat uneasy. "Who are you?" he whispered faintly.

"I didn't hear you," she followed his hand and sighed. She picked a bundle of firewood and tossed it near him. "They are ten naira each," she murmured and looked up expectantly and frowned.

Johnson pulled his shirt over his manhood and stamped his feet.

Kelechi watched him for a while and shrugged. "How many do you want?"

Realising that she was staring at his feet and not higher, he straightened. "Sorry, how much is it?"

"Ten naira, each." She muttered stiffly and tried to smile.

He quickly counted the money his mother gave him and handed it to her.

Kelechi's eyes widened, and she quickly counted her firewood.

He'd looked eagerly at her, praying he looked presentable enough to be her kind of man.

"I have only nine bundles. The rest are reserved. I don't have change now, can you come back later?"

Those were truly blessed words. To hide his excitement, he nodded.

"Thank you! Let me call okada for you?"

"Do you mind if I left them here for a while?"

Kelechi hesitated then conceded. "Okay, let's carry them near the gate or just in front."

He'd nodded. She bent down to pick a bundle.

"Oh no, don't worry, I'll carry it all," he said quickly.

She replied with a shrug. He looked rather odd in different legs of socks.

He was a little disappointed that she didn't bend down with her back turned to him again.

Just then, an okada rider rode in.

"Chi-babe!" the okada rider shouted excitedly as he rode in.

He almost passed out, suspecting the okada rider was her boyfriend.

"Abiye, good morning o!" she giggled and stepped out of his way and wiggled a finger at him. "Shebi, I don warn you."

"Chi-babe!" The okada rider repeated playfully.

She chuckled and stood akimbo beside him. "Troublemaker!"

"Eh! I 'gree! I just come tell you sey my wife don born. Your money," he said, turning off the ignition, and then he dug into his pocket and handed the naira notes to Kelechi, "the money wen you borrow me."

"Ah Abiye, thank you. Wetin she born?"

"You no go believe am o! Twins!"

"Thank God o! God don do am for you o. After five years," Kelechi did a dance. "You see, I tell you o."

"True talk, true talk," Abiye solemnly nodded.

Kelechi, still dancing, wet her thumb and began to count the money.

"Chi-babe, so na your boyfriend be this? Na im make you no gree for my brother. Na fine boy sha." He retorted just as his motorcycle roared.

Kelechi raised amused brows then looked at

Johnson, who turned to her expectantly and gave him a contemptuous frown. "No be you dey find okada?"

Abiye stopped the bike abruptly and looked at Johnson expectantly.

Disappointed, He climbed the bike with his ware in both hands hanging by his side, forgetting to discuss a price.

The following day, he took his bath early. His cousin had arrived while he was sleeping. They'd woken him twice during their banter. He was glad the second time because it gave him enough time to iron as quickly as it could go unnoticed. When the generator almost gave way, his mother shouted, and his dad went into every room to find out who was pulling the power down. Now fully dressed and not wanting to be disturbed, he locked the door and impatiently waited for an hour suitable to pay a visit.

He was, however, disappointed when he arrived to find her grandmother and not her. He stayed with her grandmother all morning, and most of the afternoon before he returned home.

The next day, he returned and found her with her grandmother. She gave him his change before he got a chance to say, 'good morning'. Her grandmother asked him to join them as they played draughts. He reluctantly turned down the offer but stayed when the old woman insisted. A customer came to buy firewood, and she left to attend to her client. Kelechi's grandmother let him win her and called out to her.

"He has won me o!"

"Eh?" Kelechi eyed her grandmother and Johnson suspiciously.

"Beginner's luck," he murmured with a shrug.

"Oya, restore my honour!" Kelechi's grandmother said, rising and patting her stool.

Kelechi frowned and said matter-of-factly, "Mama, it's only a game."

She sucked her tongue as she pulled Kelechi towards the stool. "Restore my honour!"

"Where are you going?"

"To sleep."

Johnson got up and curtsied as he bade Kelechi's grandmother goodnight.

"Good night, my son."

Kelechi shrugged. "Fine. Let's see how much of a player you really are."

"Like I said, 'beginner's luck'." His eyes twinkled with mischief. He was going to make it impossible for her to 'restore her grandmother's honour'. Exhausted, he let her win, but she noticed it and asked for a rematch the following day because she had to turn in early.

She won several times the following day because he was distracted. She asked him if he was alright, but he couldn't confide in her that he didn't dare to ask her out on a date.

A week later, he asked her out. She turned him down, offering a platonic relationship. So, he asked for her hand in marriage, but she told him to wait until he'd graduated. All he wanted was a fling, and he didn't mind waiting to add her to his list of escapades. He couldn't resist the thrill of the chase, but the day he returned from school the following year and saw her. He knew he wanted more. It was the same day he brought her to meet his parents, his mother invited her best friend's daughter to join them for dinner, and the day her grandmother kicked the bucket.

He shook his head.

He had believed that bringing her to the family home would make his mother notice her for who she was and like her. Unknown to him, his parents believed that meeting other girls outside the village was a better option and will erase Kelechi from his thoughts.

A few months after he'd graduated, his father sent an application in his stead, and he'd gained admission. They decided not to tell him until it was time for him to travel.

He came across his flight ticket when it fell out of his father's folder. It had been booked for the following day: the wedding day. If he missed his flight, the land his parents sold would be for nothing. He'd cried all night as it dawned on him that his parents really didn't want him getting married.

He hurriedly left the house to meet Kelechi. When he didn't find her at home, he went to meet the priest, Kelechi's quasi-father. A few minutes later, Kelechi and their sponsors arrived. The priest saw them and suspected they wanted a marriage blessing.

Remembering how his mother almost passed out when she found out made Johnson smile - Her nosy friends had gone to congratulate her ahead of them.

CHAPTER 10

"It's like troubled waters follow me everywhere I go with the hunger of a bloodthirsty shark," Kelechi moaned as she sobbed and recalled her wedding day.

On the eve of their wedding, Johnson's mother had promised her hell on earth if she married her son and even promised to pay her off.

Confused and desperate, she hurried to the presbytery to seek the priest. The priest had been the closest thing to a parent after the assassination of her parents. She was on her way to meet the priest when Mrs Barine and Johnson's planned sponsor stopped her, practically dragging her to her shop where they stayed fiddling with the wedding gown the woman had sewn for her.

"I don't know if I want to marry Thomas anymore," she finally admitted.

"Meaning what nawh? Anyway, it's that thing they call wedding jitters."

She shook her head.

"It is and that's that!" Mrs Barine retorted then

nursed her finger before bending down to pick up a few pins. "Get up and turn around."

Tugging at the arm of the dress, she did as she was told and grumbled. "His mother hates me."

"Don't they all?" Mrs Barine said through clenched teeth holding the pins between them.

Kelechi straightened her back. "But this is different."

"It's your first time. She will grow to love you."

Kelechi shook her head again. "You won't understand, she came to see me yesterday."

"What?" Mrs Barine yelped, discarding the pins that she'd held with her teeth and quickly spun Kelechi to face her.

"Aww!" Kelechi yelped when some pins pricked her foot.

"Sorry! Ew, sorry o!" Mrs Barine discarded the pincushion so she could talk freely as she picked the pins on the ground with a magnet. "What did she want?"

"She promised to make my life miserable if I married her son."

"Why didn't she warn her son?" Mrs Barine retorted blandly.

She shrugged. She'd been wondering why herself.

"Remember, it was last week that the last of the bans of marriage was read. Ignore her! Just because she is the president of CWO she now

thinks everyone should bow to her like those sycophants in Saint Anne's group."

"You still don't understand."

"Quit whining and stay steady." Mrs Barine mumbled as she tucked another edge of the sleeve of Kelechi's wedding gown. "If that woman wants your relationship with her son to end, then she can meet Father Jude with her reasons and stop acting like a coward."

Kelechi sighed. Nobody understood what she was going through. She knew the woman was serious, and she hated tension and, worst of all, one with a mother-in-law. She didn't have someone to run to. Abiye had once told her that he believed that it was a woman's job to secure her place in a man's life, but she knew it was more. Since her parents' death, she'd been taken advantage of. It was easier to just be on her own.

Kelechi closed her eyes to hold back tears. *She'd promised her grandmother that she'd be a good wife to Johnson, but weren't promises meant to be broken? Her grandmother had predicted this outcome because she said trials would come in various forms. Was this one of them? Why should cheating be an expected outcome?*

She grimaced as her mind returned to her wedding day.

She smoothed her hand over the soft lace and

let Mrs Barine tug the back of the dress. She wanted it loose, but Mrs Barine said: 'You only wear it once' as she made it snug. The words of her soon-to-be mother-in-law echoed in her head several times. Although Father Jude had asked her to see him after Mass, she couldn't wait. She tried her best to sit still, not knowing how long she'd been sitting there until the bells pealed. She got up abruptly and started heading towards the presbytery.

"Wait! Chi, wait! I never comot the pin finish o!" Mrs Barine exclaimed.

"I'm coming!" Kelechi's voice echoed over the wind.

"Where you dey go?" Mrs Barine asked as she quickly tucked her feet into her sandal and chased Kelechi, still holding a large pair of scissors and a pincushion.

Kelechi was determined to see Father Jude and would have been running but for the restrictive gown.

Mrs Barine continued running after her.

When they got to Father Jude's house, the catechist didn't allow her in. While she dallied, Mrs Barine caught up with her and started removing the pins and cutting threads.

"Chairman Sir, good morning," the catechist murmured cheerfully and began to open the gate when a bicycle stopped.

"Mrs Barine," the cyclist called as he got off his bicycle.

Mrs Barine murmured her greeting as she rushed in after Kelechi while the cyclist shook hands with the catechist.

As Kelechi knocked on the door of the presbytery, Mrs Barine fiddled with her dishevelled appearance.

"Mrs Barine, what's the hurry? What happened?" the cyclist asked, just as the priest opened the door. He was already fully dressed except for his chasuble

"Good morning Father!" they all chorused.

"Good morning all. Come in," Father Jude retorted excitedly, opened the door wider and stepped aside to let them in.

She froze when she found Johnson in the sitting room, looking downcast. "Are you okay?" she finally asked, moving towards him.

Dumbfounded, Johnson turned away. "I'm not supposed to see you in your wedding gown until after the wedding."

The cyclist and Mrs Barine laughed, and the priest frowned at what Johnson had said before exiting the sitting room. Johnson got up to greet them.

"Why are you here so early?" The cyclist asked, holding Johnson's hand and pulling him away from the women.

"There is a problem. My flight ticket is for tomorrow, and I'm supposed to leave for the airport in the afternoon."

They looked back at the women, Kelechi plopped onto a sofa and abruptly got up. Mrs Barine rushed to her side to search the pin.

"Thomas, your traditional marriage is for tomorrow evening," the cyclist quipped in a loud whisper.

Johnson nodded.

Kelechi knew something was wrong when she saw Johnson in Father Jude's house. She watched the cyclist pull Johnson aside and knew it was bad. Perhaps this union was not meant to be. She glared at the wedding gown and sniggered. They hadn't even bought the wedding rings. To distract herself, she decided to count the intricate details of the lace.

"Your mother planned all this," Mrs Barine spoke matter-of-factly, standing beside them.

The cyclist glared at her. He scratched his bald head for a few seconds and then began to play with his beard. After a while, his eyes glistened. "You may as well get married today."

"What?" Johnson asked. "How?"

Mrs Barine looked on expectantly at the cyclist.

"Kelechi is dressed the part, you're formally dressed. My wife and I are decently dressed..."

the cyclist gestured at Mrs Barine.

Mrs Barine nodded in agreement as she adjusted her dress.

Kelechi shook her head dismissively.

Mrs Barine pinched her and whispered. "It's meant to be."

Just then, Father Jude walked in with a shopping bag. He dug into it and produced a small box. Smiling, he handed the box to Johnson and the shopping bag to Kelechi. She clumsily opened one of the boxes in the bag, opened it, and gasped.

"Thank you, Father." She sighed and bit her lower lip to prevent herself from crying.

"I couldn't think of a better gift to give you for giving me the privilege of officiating my first wedding."

While the priest was still speaking, Johnson opened the box he was given to reveal wedding bands.

Mrs Barine clapped gleefully, murmuring, "It's meant to be. See, I told you."

"It's the least I could do."

"I guess you're ready for a marriage blessing."

"Yes, they are!" The cyclist said before Johnson or Kelechi could respond.

"I thought so." Father Jude said, nodding.

"You did?" Mrs Barine asked.

"As soon as I saw all of you here, I knew." He

pondered briefly and frowned at Johnson. "Where are your parents?"

"They may arrive really late," The cyclist said quickly and twisted his mouth.

Mrs Barine looked at the cyclist proudly and nodded.

"Is that true?" Father Jude asked Johnson raising a warning hand at the cyclist.

"It's true," Johnson muttered.

Kelechi didn't know how to react to everything, so she merely watched the proceeding. She almost interrupted them and remembered what her grandmother had asked her just before giving them her blessings: "do you love him?"

During Mass that morning, they exchanged marital vows.

She hesitated during the exchange, but the eagerness in Johnson's eyes, the urgency in Mr and Mrs Barine's gestures, and the promise in her grandmother's words quelled her fears. At that moment, he was all she cared about, and in their excitement, they went to inform his parents.

But they'd already been made aware of it and locked her and Johnson out. So, they took the festivity to Mr and Mrs Barine's house.

Kelechi sighed, toying with her wedding band. She still hurt from the fact that he didn't acknowledge her and the way he held the other woman. A stranger. The way the other woman reacted to her husband's touch, a privilege she had deprived herself of because she valued chastity in marriage. She had been married to him for close to ten years, and she didn't have a child to show for it. *How could I conceive if my husband does not touch me? How can I see past this?*

The real change she wanted was to get pregnant. But first, she must have something to fall back on. Something like money.

How else would I take care of a child?

She decided to get a contraceptive.

Just until I have an income, she promised.

CHAPTER 11

Johnson frowned when he heard something drop through the letter box. Fuming, he went to investigate what Stella had ordered again and found

a lumpy, battered envelope. He tore it open as he made his way to the loo. He was in tears a few minutes later. The envelope was filled with pictures that showed his wife's maltreatment by his parents and cousins. The letter was dated five years ago. He opened the rumpled papers; it was four sheets of lined papers. He sobbed silently as he read the details of his wife's torture. Father Jude had helped her gain admission into the polytechnic before he moved to Rome.

He wiped his face and read it again.

This letter was given to Maurice five years ago! Five years ago!

There was a short note attached to the post it. It was from Maurice's wife; it explained that she went through the bin after her husband stealthily tossed something into it. Outraged and annoyed that she'd held onto something so horrific, something that concerned his happiness, he decided to disregard helping her. Maurice was supposed to be his ally. Now he had cause to believe that the rumours of his hitting on Kelechi were true.

It was his sincere belief that living with his parents would make them see his wife for who she really was and love her like they would love a daughter. His mother's allegations hurt the most. He knew his mother didn't like Kelechi but was shocked at the level of maltreatment meted on her. It hurt him so much so he began to re-evaluate being responsible for her care.

His mother had told him that Kelechi was sleeping around, but he didn't blame her and had decided to forgive her because she had told him before he left the country that she wouldn't wait after four years. He had hoped that she would because she was a very careful and judicious person. But she was also a hardworking, beautiful woman that any man would die for. Besides, she never wrote to him or responded to his letters.

What if Kelechi wasn't a virgin? He always trusted his mother and not the one person he should have.

Johnson remained in the toilet as he wept. Remembering the only letter he had received from Kelechi, gave him an understanding of why she consented, she was tired and angry.

CHAPTER 12

As Kelechi's tears expired, she went to the kitchen sink to wash her face. She had felt her husband's member stir. She had longed for him and even felt heat rise in her, but she was angry at seeing a woman on her husband, albeit a woman who shared her title.

She leaned on the windowsill as she remembered what it felt like being with him, shuddered with excitement, and sighed. Fiddling around the tap, she pondered on her future. At the same time, she heard the clap of the letter box. She hoped it was the letter she was expecting from her cousin as he'd promised to call as soon as he had gotten a new place to stay. She stretched her hand to open the door and held her breath when she heard her husband's footfall. She'd promised to put her emotions in check when he was around and failed yet again.

She took in a few breaths to compose herself and made her way to the door. A fleeting glance revealed her husband sitting on the bed bent over a parcel.

*

Johnson saw his wife tiptoe towards the door and smiled. He was going to make it impossible for her to ignore or shy away from him. He just had to find a way to make it impossible for her to lock the bedroom door. He wrinkled his face and pondered.

If I do, Stella will want the bedroom back. Kelechi would have no respite.

He scratched his head.

If she doesn't let me in, how will I make it up to her? I can't afford to push her away nor let her stay away.

It was moments like this that he hated himself because he couldn't make up his mind; moments when ideas came and went like the weather, yet none tangible.

*

They'd run out of flour, baking powder, sugar, and her new favourite, chocolate spread. Glad to have an excuse to leave the house, Kelechi picked up her jacket, emptied Johnson's wallet again, and went out nodding to herself.

Forgetting her phone, she returned to the room for her phone then heard Johnson's raised voice and inched closer to the bedroom door. She frowned, wondering if she should be listening, but it was with his mother; it was about her and pictures Father Jude had sent him.

Leaning against the wall, she listened in on her husband as he read the letter Father Jude had written to him. She was astounded that Father Jude had known that she'd been lying to him about her welfare. That he was proud of her formidable strength and resilience gave her some comfort. She wiped her tears and made a solemn promise to call Father Jude the following day.

Now, more than ever, she needed to step out of the house for a breath of fresh air. Not having any friends to relate with, Kelechi planned to sleep in on Christmas day as she didn't want to cross paths with her husband or Stella. It was two days away and she wanted to be prepared. She went out to buy what she'd need to stash for her enshrouded days. As she passed by a charity shop, she spotted a red dress and went into the shop and tried it on, but it was too tight.

She tried on other dresses and settled for a scoop neck velvet dress in royal blue, a short-sleeved hoodie, and a one-shoulder dress with loads of ruffles, and these were too large giving her ideas on alterations. Realising that she didn't have enough money to satisfy her sweet tooth if she got a book, she moaned. But the novels called to her, especially when she found most of her favourite authors on display.

As she was leaving the shop, something struck

her on the face. Frowning as her vision turned cloudy, she saw a man pointing at her and gesturing at his ware and cussed in an unfamiliar language. Another man, much taller, screeched to a halt in front of her, apologizing and gesturing. A little boy came to stand by the tall man with arms wrapped around a ball.

She swatted the taller man's hand as she tried to hold back tears from the hurt. Her nose was bleeding. She staggered and was caught by the same man. She could feel herself move, but she couldn't see past the pain she was experiencing. The woman who had just cautioned the little boy brought a stool to her and pulled her head back. The smell of nail polish assured her that she was in a salon.

"No, no no, wrong way," the same man cautioned with a sharp voice. "Please bring your first aid kit," he finished and squatted in front of her as he made her lean forward, lifting her hand to her nose.

The woman murmured into Kelechi's face. "I no get o!"

"Go buy abeg! You get pikin and you no get first aid kit?" the man with the offending hand asked, more to himself, and then murmured something under his breath in Ogoni language.

Kelechi laughed at the way he said the parable.

"I know that laugh anywhere. You can open

your eyes now."

"Igoni?" she asked when she opened her eyes.

"One and only," Igoni struck his chest and opened his arms.

She chuckled then tried to blow her nose.

He touched her arms and cautioned. "Don't sniff, don't blow."

She wrinkled her nose. "What makes you an expert?"

"Experience."

She chuckled again.

"What are you doing here?" he asked. He patted her knee as he rose, creating a shadow over her.

She shrugged.

"Still mysterious, eh?" he asked, grinning.

"You, what are you doing here?" She asked, slanting her head to take a better look at him.

He pointed at the woman who just walked in and shoved a first aid kit at him. "My cousin, she owns this place. I drop by anytime I visit London. Enough about me, what have you been doing? Where are you staying?"

"Behind." She replied grimly and smoothed her hands on her dress.

"You live in Edgware?"

"Behind, as in behind me."

He frowned at her as she gestured. He squinted briefly, then his eyes widened with understanding. "On this street? Oh my, this is a lovely coincidence."

Kelechi noticed that she was getting comfortable with Igoni, way too comfortable. She removed the handkerchief from her nose, felt her nose gently, and straightened. "True. Thanks, but I have to leave."

"Do I still scare you?"

Taken aback, she asked. "Scare me?"

"Yeah. You're always in a hurry after a few talks. I won't detain you though. Your phone number, please?" He pleaded; his eyes undressed her.

"I don't know my number." She said quickly, hesitantly producing her phone.

He stretched his hand to her. "Let me give you mine."

She gave it to him and got up carrying her bag with her.

"Don't forget to save my number though," he warned, his eyes dancing roguishly.

She nodded. Sighing heavily, she made her way back home, struggling not to look back. Unknown to her, the boy whose ball had landed on her face was following her.

It's been four years already, she smiled thoughtfully, shaking her head. *Igoni.* He'd been her strength and almost her weakness probably because he reminded her Johnson. He had stronger features, which she thought was too square. But she loved his thin, raspy voice. She sniggered as she remembered when they first met.

It was a week after matriculation. She and Simisola had gone to Simisola's brother's house – that was what she'd thought at the time - until Simisola began to undress in front of the man, and he practically dragged Simisola to his room. She would have left Simisola if they hadn't spent the last of their money travelling to meet Simisola's 'brother'.

The man gave her excess money for transport and his business card while he ogled her. Disgusted, she didn't wait for Simisola as she rushed out and hailed an okada. She arrived at the room Simisola shared with Baridakara, knocked and walked in before realising that there was a young man in the room.

That young man was Igoni. He was dating Baridakara at the time. However, she walked in on him smooching Dumlesi, Baridakara's cousin. They quickly separated, but she'd seen enough. Dumlesi was the opposite of rude that day, so much so she began to feel smothered.

From that day, Igoni hung around her everywhere she went. He was fun to be with and a distraction from what she was going through with her in-laws. They fast became best friends. He made her the first and only person to celebrate her birthday in the classroom.

Smiling at the memory, she made a mental note to ask about the pictures. Hesitantly, she turned and caught sight of their neighbour dragging a Christmas tree up the stairs and frowned. She was sure the woman was Muslim. She had to learn the mind-your-business rule in England as her cousin had advised, but it was tempting to know why she had a Christmas tree.

The house was quiet when she got in. It was only when she got into the kitchen that she saw the sticky note her husband had left her. There was no need as he was going to be out for less than an hour - a nice touch on his part. It would not, however, make up for what she had seen.

She baked late into the night. She only found out it was 2am when Stella returned from work. She knew Stella would eat up the cake if she left them all in the fridge – the chocolate cake she found was Stella's favourite. With no real hiding place for them, she split them, a layer she left in the oven, another in the fridge, and left the kitchen with the rest.

Fatigue had finally seeped into her bones, so when she got the room and tucked her feet under the duvet and barely pulled up when Stella's snoring tore into the quiet night. Johnson was a light sleeper. Kelechi had known no one who snored as loudly as Stella when she was drunk. It was weird that drinking made her snore, but it was a good punishment for him. She dreaded seeing her husband's arms around another woman, and Stella would be up in a few hours.

Kelechi slapped her forehead. She'd forgotten to do her husband's laundry and sniggered. She'd been too angry to take advantage of her opportunities too. She roused herself from the bed, willing her legs to take the necessary steps and her mind to be strengthened with a bigger picture.

Holding her breath, she walked to the bathroom and carried the laundry basket to the kitchen. On getting there, she found her husband bent over the oven door.

Johnson jumped, hitting his head on the cabinet door he'd left open. He hadn't heard her come in. "I..." he started to explain then thinned his lips.

Kelechi didn't look at him; she squatted in front of the washing machine. She wasn't going to let him get under her skin, so she concentrated on sorting the clothes.

"Nwunye'm, can't we at least try to be civil?" he asked, whispering.

Kelechi let out a long hiss.

Johnson sighed. He'd been giving up easily but not this time. He wasn't going to let her keep him out. "You know I have to do this."

Kelechi glared at him.

"I didn't have a choice!"

Unable to contain her anger anymore, she responded. "You did! You chose the easy way. You even dared to let her... Another woman on top of my husband, in the living room that's supposed to be ours." Stopping to catch her breath, she tightened her grip on the washing machine.

"Do you know that she shares the -"

"Shares what? Do you think you're the only man with a penis?"

"Nwunye'm!" he admonished.

"I'm not done talking," she squeaked, her breathing ragged. She struck her chest to ease the pain that clouded it, but it wouldn't give. She could no longer stand and had to lean over the cabinet by the sink. Johnson came to soothe her, but she forcefully shoved him away. "You've caused me more pain than happiness. From the day I married you I've only known pain, that's all you've given, that's all you've got to offer."

Johnson froze.

The first set of clothes had been set on a quick wash. She brought them out, and gingerly pushed the second one in. Johnson touched her hand. She pulled her hand away as if scalded. She didn't bother to turn on the machine but left with the wet clothes.

Stella chose that time to change position,

revealing her pert buttocks.

Kelechi hissed and spat on the carpet, not caring, and hoped her husband stepped on it. She began to weep and quickly locked the bathroom door, crumbling on the wet clothes she'd just washed. She was tired of crying, but the tears came with ease. It seemed to wash away the pain, albeit briefly, so she let it continue, not holding back.

CHAPTER 13

Johnson frowned Johnson turned the washing machine on and was ready to go to her. He could hear sobbing and almost ran to the bathroom. As he stretched his hand to knock on the door, Stella stopped him.

"Why is she crying?" Stella murmured through sleep-laden eyes.

"I don't know," Johnson coughed.

"I bet you don't."

"What do you think?" he asked, feigning innocence.

"I didn't realise we were friends?" Stella said sarcastically and added softly. "When she is ready to talk about it. She'll let you in."

Johnson, trying to find out what she'd heard, asked, "How long has she been crying?"

"Dunno, she woke me up just as she did you. Let's sleep."

"I've got to work." He said quickly.

Stella laughed dreamily. "You're only saying that because I snore. It's okay. You can sleep later, you always do."

Just then, her phone rang. She stretched her hand towards it, but Johnson had seen the message on the screen. It read: 'this discussion is far from over...' He couldn't see the rest of the message without opening the phone. He'd never bothered to ask for the password. At that moment, it was all he wanted to do.

To distract himself, Johnson produced his laptop. After staring at the screen for almost an hour, he closed the laptop and stared blankly at the window.

What have I gotten myself into?

He'd known stress and had been able to battle it, but this stress was a different kind, the type he couldn't shelf, bin or run away from. It lingered leeringly. Now, as he sat in the dark room in the blackness before sunrise, he wondered if he had been acting selfishly all these years. Kelechi had been right when she said he wasn't the only one who had a penis. She'd waited, weathering every storm his family had presented her. He was her first. His parents had told him malicious lies about his wife. He believed them and decided to soothe his pride by turning to the arms of any willing woman. She'd been told lies about him, yet she remained steadfast, what did that make him?

Perhaps, it was truly all about him. He wanted to stay and make money and go back to show her he'd made it. He hadn't made any plans beyond that because he loved her. Seeing her in pain hurt so much, there weren't words to describe it. How unfortunate that she had to find out the way she did. She was somewhat vindictive. She had surprised him by doing nothing to hurt him or Stella except deprive him of her body, which was of more value to him than anything else. He nodded his gratitude to God that she changed then grimaced.

The one day in the week that he could be with her exclusively, she'd withdrawn. He hoped he hadn't caused her to lose her faith because he no longer heard her say the Rosary. She just remained locked up in the room, hardly coming out except to use the toilet. He was sure she was hiding food in the room's little fridge. He'd been in the room the day before reading Father Jude's letter. It smelt so heavenly that he decided to wait for her, unaware that she'd left the house.

The washing machine beeped; Johnson groaned as it reminded him of seeing her in the lingerie, he'd bought her.

He raised a puzzled brow; *did she wear it to entice me? That would mean her anger was a farce. No! Her pain was as real as the rising sun.*

He groaned again, glowering at his stirring manhood.

Kelechi, if this is torture on your part, it's working.

He closed his eyes and exhaled, trying to rid his mind of his wife in the lingerie, but it came back like the stubborn mosquito. He groaned again.

"Hi!" Stella murmured as she hugged him.

He groaned again, this time inwardly as his manhood lost its desire to be felt. He frowned as the stench of stale beer escaped from Stella's mouth. He thought of telling her off, but her phone began to ring. Still holding his breath, he got up and made his way to the bathroom, leaving her no choice but to get her phone. A few minutes later, he heard a knock on the door.

"You heard me knock," Stella growled. "Open the darn door! You know I've got to work today."

He flushed the toilet, quickly applied toothpaste to his toothbrush then opened the door. Stella rushed in, causing the door to swing back. Johnson stepped aside just in time as he was used to her in-a-rush routine. Unfortunately, this time it left a dent in the wall, Johnson's heart sank as he remembered his deposit. More so, it reminded him that his rent was due.

"Stella..." he groaned and gestured at the damaged wall.

"Oh no! I'll fix it, I promise." She pleaded as she peered in the mirror for any facial imperfections. Satisfied, she continued with her routine.

He watched her, wincing as she squeezed the toothpaste from the middle, then run the toothbrush under the tap. He chuckled. *Was there a need for it? Your mouth is already moist*. He sighed ruefully; he missed kissing Kelechi. *Why should a woman have such an effect on a man like him?* He looked back at the wall and shook his head as he made his way out of the bathroom.

Kelechi looked at him for a few seconds as she returned to the room, locking the door behind her.

He angrily stalked into the living room, deciding that he would take the door out. He paced for a while before slumping onto the sofa bed. Glancing at the coffee mug he'd left on the table, he gritted his teeth and gurgled the cold liquid. The table brought back memories that caused him grief but left a smile on his face. He'd never noticed the size of the table until he made love to Kelechi on it. It used to be an eyesore until it fell under her charm.

She had organised it in such a way that he could place his A3 paper without struggling or scouting for space. She had helped create a working space by removing almost everything from the small round table. The textbooks she placed underneath the table in a hard card box with one side cut up to show off their titles. Small items lined the right side of the table, a hand-painted yoghurt pot in which she stored his pencils and pens. Beside it, a paint-splattered paperweight, a discoloured fountain globe, a broken card catalogue, a pencil tin filled with pins; and, a scented candle in musk and cognac which he'd been searching for for a long time. He'd meant to ask her where she got the quirky paperweight.

His anger had dissipated, giving way for a mundane feeling. Crestfallen, he stared morosely at the items on the table. Having nothing sobering, he decided to watch a movie. Like dust entering his eyes, he shook his head and peered at the arrangement at the side of the table set against the wall and guffawed. In front of him lay the design he'd been racking his brain for.

Giggling, he discarded the laptop on the chair beside him and then tried to wedge his cascading pencils and spread an A3 sheet on the table at the same time. He was oblivious of Stella who'd just returned from the bathroom, clad in a towel.

Stella raised a brow and then smiled, discarding her towel on the chair with the laptop on it. She went into the kitchen, wiggling her buttock. She came back, but he didn't seem to notice her, so she did her version of a rhythmic dance as she sauntered towards him.

He quickly picked up a ruler, untucked the pencil and drew lines as the idea for the quirky building that could further secure his position at the company continued to unravel in his head.

Seeing this, Stella halted for a second then

proceeded to give him a neck massage, but seeing that his response wasn't welcoming, she let go, pointing at his A3 paper and murmured, "Killjoy".

Relieved and glad for the little distraction, which gave him an additional idea, he finished the framework by noon. Excited and hungry, he crunched his fingers and went to the kitchen to find something to settle his stomach's complaint.

As he opened the fridge, he remembered Kelechi baking most of last night and lost his appetite. Not because he didn't like her baking or cooking; it was the fact that she never complained that clawed at him. After everything she'd gone through with his parents, he didn't deserve her kindness.

There was always a home-cooked meal in the house. His clothes were ironed. He ironed Stella's to avert suspicion. The house was always spotless except the area around the TV and sofas – he and Stella's undoing. It looked like a well-maintained golf course bordered by a dumpsite. Sometimes he suspected that Stella did it to spite him for not hiring a cleaner because she wasn't untidy when they met. He had never asked Kelechi how she got the money until he went through his wallet. Stella would instead take his card so that he doesn't discover how much she'd spent until too late. Both women were sapping his strength in their own way. Still, he made a mental note to replace the funds in his wallet.

He glanced around the kitchen and sighed. Determined to talk to Kelechi whether she liked it or not, he shut the door of the fridge and went to knock on the bedroom door. Luckily for him, she was coming out of the room; he hid until she was inside the bathroom, then went into the room to wait for her behind the door. As he did, he was overwhelmed with the need to pace. He decided to counter this urge by tapping his fingers lightly on the door and stopped when he heard the shower go off.

He held his breath for fear that any reaction on his path would deter her from entering the room. She was taking a long time to come out, and when she finally did, she went into the sitting room and turned back halfway and went to the bedroom. As soon as she got in, he shut the door behind them and exhaled heavily. She was about to undo the towel and stopped and turned to face him. She laughed so hard she had to hug herself to soothe the emerging discomfort.

"You're laughing at my pain, I'm glad," Johnson said, still catching his breath and shaking of the numbness in his legs.

She sniggered and began to cream her body. "You don't know pain."

Dreamy-eyed, he watched her hands move under the towel and fell to his knees.

How can a mere woman have this effect on me?

Panting, he shook his head.

She is no mere woman. She is my wife.

His manhood nodded in agreement. On his knees, he moved closer to her and stifled a groan when she rested a foot on the bed and began to smooth the lotion on it. His eyes glazed, and he did something he'd never had the courage to do with any other woman. He pressed his lips to her vulva and the rest as they say.

CHAPTER 14

Kelechi watched her husband as he languorously lay beside her. Remembering how he'd mentioned that she was *too conservative,* she wanted to try something new. She had an idea but dreaded initiating it so much so that he fell asleep and woke up, and she still couldn't make a move. A little boldness came when she recalled that Stella would return soon.

She tentatively untied the lace of his jogging bottoms and gingerly touched his manhood.

"Tell me how you like it?"

Johnson, unsure of what he wanted and feeling he didn't deserve the pleasure of her generosity, shook his head.

Not receiving a response from him, she decided to rely on Simisola's suggestion.

Taking deep breaths, she started. Curiosity and eagerness propelled her as she gave his manhood long and slow strokes. Swayed by her husband's reaction to her touch, she brought his phallus out of the jogging bottoms and knelt in front of him, but her nerves got the best of her on seeing it pulsate. She looked up at him again but wavered when she saw his eyes closed. His moaning gave her the confidence she needed. Pride surged through her at pleasing her husband so.

In no long time, he was chanting her name, and she welled with pride. She figured it was only a matter of time before he'd be eating off her fingers. If things went according to plan, she would have the child she desperately wanted, and if there was nothing else for her in their marriage, then so be it.

Let's see another woman please you like I do.

It was Saturday.

Stella was out as always, except much earlier.

Kelechi went out of the room briefly and returned with a platter and two glasses. She sighed when she returned to find him still splayed languorously on the bed. She was going to be that patient dog that ate the fastest bone, and she was going to be as cunning as the serpent. Smiling, she climbed into the bed beside him.

Johnson wrapped his arms around her and turned her to face him.

"Just hear me out," he started. "I'm sorry about what you went through with my family, what I've put you through and what I'm putting you through."

She tried to fight the tears that were about to flow, but it flowed regardless. She curled up to him and cried. He was all she had. She admitted for the first time that she was afraid of trying anything new. Except for Igoni, but Igoni was a breath of fresh air as a friend. She shook her head and tried to turn away.

Johnson tightened his hold and wiped her eyes. “Are you okay?”

Nodding, she decided to investigate her problem because it had just dawned on her that Johnson wasn’t the only contention.

She was quite distracted and didn’t notice Johnson move until he began to caress her. As desire slithered to her toes. *Oh, this husband of mine is going to be the death of me,* she thought as she moaned, giggled, gasped, and whimpered, welcoming the sensation his touch singed on her skin.

CHAPTER 15

Kelechi and Johnson had spent the rest of Saturday and the whole of Sunday in bed, only leaving when they had to and this they did together. Kelechi didn't think it was a good idea to stay in bed on a Monday, but it was, after all, Christmas day. Kelechi woke up early and cooked so much food that there was no space to store them. She was about to get into the bathroom when she heard the door. A note had been slipped through the letterbox. Kelechi erased the swear words that littered the letter from her mind as she read it:

> *JT,*
> *What happened to your phone? I called Maurice last night, and he hadn't seen you. I don't know what's going on with you. I quite frankly do not care. I'll be back by 1 pm. If I don't find this door unlocked, I will break it down.*

"Who was it?" Johnson asked from inside the bathroom.

"No one!" Kelechi shouted a little too cheerfully and quickly crushed the paper and walked back to the kitchen. He waylaid her and smothered her with kisses before letting her go then pulled her away to scrutinize her.

"Are you okay?"

"Yep," she sighed. "I thought I smelt burning food."

"Oh, okay," he let her go after massaging her buttocks. "Don't be long!"

She smiled and rushed to the kitchen. It was the one time she regretted emptying the bin. She quickly tore the paper, wet it, and was about to toss it into the food bin when Johnson strode into the kitchen and wrapped his arms around her waist. She stiffened.

"Are you sure you're okay?" he murmured into her neck.

She steered him towards the sink to rinse her hand. "Mh-huh."

"Join me, please." He murmured, not waiting for a response as he gently ushered her out of the kitchen.

Kelechi watched the last of the sludgy papers spin through the drain then smiled as she murmured in her most sultry voice. "With pleasure."

They arrived late to church. Fortunately, they weren't the only ones. Zainab and Áyò were late too. An hour after they'd returned from the church, there was a knock on the door. Kelechi, thinking it was Stella and company, reluctantly left her husband's side and went to the room.

Johnson looked at the time, hoping Stella and her friends weren't drunk as he didn't want to spend money on taxi fare. However, he opened the door and chewed his teeth. Maurice and Kelechi's friends had come. He was not pleased to see Maurice, but he kept his cool because of the women. Stepping aside to let them in and briefly went out to get drinks while the women distracted Maurice. Luckily, Kelechi had cooked for the sake of cooking. He was glad it wouldn't go to waste.

A few minutes after he'd returned, Stella's friends arrived to take their friend out.

Kelechi heard a familiar voice and went to peer through the window. It was Stella's red-haired friend.

Johnson frowned at them in confusion when he didn't find Stella in their midst. "Is Stella, alright?"

The women looked at each other and looked at him.

"Was that a trick question?" Portia asked, tucking her sunglasses in her bag. "Andi, my phone please?"

"What's going on here?" Johnson asked.

Kelechi listened in as she'd never heard Johnson take that tone with anyone. A part of her wanted to join him, but she decided against it and changed her dress instead.

"We should be asking you the same," Andi said as she handed her phone to Portia.

"What have you done with our friend?" The third girl asked

"I better call the police!" Andi dramatically ransacked her bag, even though she'd just given Portia her phone.

"Let us in. We must talk to Stella now," Portia said frowning.

Johnson closed the door behind him. "Oh no, you're not entering my house."

"Your house," The third girl sniggered, pulling her trench coat around her tiny frame.

"I will call the police," Andi said pointedly.

"What are you waiting for?" Johnson asked, leaning on the door frame as he crossed his arms. "I want you to call the police so you can explain to them why Stella would leave her husband's side on Saturday for work and a party you're supposed to have been to and not returned."

Andi laughed sarcastically. "That's impossible..."

"She means Stella never came to the party,"

Portia added quietly. "And we've got no deadlines, so no overtime."

"What!?" Johnson asked and fell back on the door.

Maurice opened the door Johnson was leaning on. Simisola, Zainab, and Áyò came out. Kelechi seized this opportunity to join the group, locking the bedroom behind her and slipping the key into her bra, so she didn't forget where it was.

"What's going on?" Maurice asked as he joined the group at the door.

Stella coincidentally arrived looking flushed and in a different outfit than she left the house in. It seemed her friends had an opinion about him and Johnson, incensed by her friends' vague accusation, didn't let her in.

Seeing her, Kelechi decided it was time to play hostess. It was then that Maurice noticed her.

Seeing Kelechi, Stella's friends resolved to let themselves into the house.

"Where are you coming from?" Johnson asked, blocking her path.

Stella ignored him and tried to get around him.

He shut the door behind him. "Where are you coming from?"

"It's Christmas Day, and I don't want to fight." Stella mused through clenched teeth.

He raised a brow. "And I want one?"

All the women except Simisola and Andi were

now leaning on the door, eavesdropping. Simisola and Andi were all over Maurice. Maurice enjoyed the attention, but he fixated on Kelechi. She walked into the sitting room wearing a halter-neck white dress with a pleated skirt that stopped just below the knees, revealing her endless legs. It was only then that Simisola and Andi realised that the other girls were missing. Andi went in search of the girls and frowned when she found four girls huddled at the door with their ears pressed to it but was distracted by her ringing phone. She left the hallway and went into the bathroom. Simisola took her spot watching the other women, playing with her necklace.

Maurice stealthily tiptoed to the kitchen.

Kelechi was bent over the oven, checking the chicken and jumped when someone held her by the waist. She didn't notice anyone come in and hissed when she saw who it was.

"So, when did you get into the country?" Maurice asked, leaning against the counter closest to her, boxing her in.

Her instinct told her that it was best to have no communication with him. "Go to the sitting room. I'll bring the drinks myself."

"I can help myself. And you haven't answered my question."

Kelechi sucked and pursed her lips.

"Do you know how pretty you are when you do

that?" Maurice asked and moved closer to her.

She still found him revolting. *Who on earth goes after his friend's wife?* "Maurice, step back." She ordered. *Being married hasn't changed him.*

"Why? Why would I want to step away from such beauty as yourself?"

"I meant what I said. Stay away from me!" Kelechi sniped.

He chuckled and still came close. The only thing close to her hand was the empty bottle of wine in the sink. She grasped it the way Igoni had taught her and swiped it at his head. Just then Simisola, Stella and Andi walked in. Maurice hadn't noticed them and raised his hand to slap her when two people shouted behind him. He hurriedly left the kitchen and brushed past his friend without stopping.

"Hey, Maurice, wetin happen?" Johnson asked, surprised.

Kelechi ran past Johnson towards the bedroom, tugging at the door, forgetting that she'd hidden the key. Simisola caught up with her after she retrieved it, and they entered the room together. Simisola locked the door just before Stella and Andi caught up with them.

"What is going on?" Johnson asked, staring at them, but his question was directed at Stella.

Andi opened her mouth to speak, but Stella poked her. "I'll tell you later."

Johnson frowned, suspecting Stella must have said something to annoy Kelechi. If she did, he would deal with her. A voice in his thoughts laughed saying, *do what?*

The rest of the day Johnson waited for Kelechi and Simisola to come out of the bedroom, but none of them did.

Simisola, knowing that Kelechi wanted to be alone, set up a movie channel for her, and left a little after.

Stella let out a long, slow sigh of relief anytime Johnson's phone rang as she didn't want him to discover how tense she was. She had noticed how irritable he'd been and suspected he wasn't satisfied with her explanation.

She still hadn't figured out a perfect excuse for where she'd been for the past two days. She twisted her mouth, pondering. Johnson wouldn't understand the fact that she had no choice. Her mother had a huge appetite for the luxuries of life. Her parents were mortgaged to the hilt. Neither she nor Johnson could afford it. That's where Henry came in.

That's the excuse she'd told herself for years. How could she admit that she married Johnson to spite Henry for marrying Megan, the girl he'd cheated on her with? He had promised that it was nothing at the time. She'd ended things with him a year before she married Johnson. She hadn't expected to see Henry again. Fate had brought them together through her job – the company belonged to his father.

She slanted her eyes and saw the dates she'd circled on the calendar and winced. She'd been so distracted lately. She couldn't tell Johnson that she was pregnant knowing how adamant he was about not wanting a baby until they were financially stable. She hadn't used protection with Henry Hopkins in the past two months. More so, Johnson had been careful.

She wasn't ready for a baby either, so she had to get rid of it. This was going to be the second abortion in less than three months, and she'd promised herself to get on the contraception. But because her friends were always with her, she couldn't possibly leave without an explicit account of where she was going.

Henry wasn't ready either. He'd promised to stop the cash flow if she did. Sometimes she wondered what she wanted. She was sure it wasn't a baby bump.

"If Johnson was beginning to suspect, then he was several years too late," she only hoped Johnson wouldn't call her mother because the woman didn't know when to keep her mouth shut.

She looked at her ringing phone and groaned

inwardly.

This is Christmas Day, for goodness sake!

She looked up and saw Johnson heading to the kitchen and quickly ran to the bathroom with her phone and locked herself in.

Kelechi had no desire to see anyone, but her bladder was about to burst. She hurriedly stretched her hand and was about to turn the knob when she heard.

"Call me and pretend to be my dad... well, come up with something. I'll need a few days to rest to avoid suspicion," Stella whispered sternly.

Hissing, Kelechi knocked.

"Come on!" Stella groaned, staring at her phone at the toilet bowl for a while, then she opened the door and glared at Kelechi as she brushed past Kelechi.

Kelechi wanted to sit down, noticed something black and almost jump out of her skin before recognising that it was Stella's phone. She must have startled Stella, but that didn't annoy her; what did was the fact that she had blown her chance of being alone with her husband for a couple of days. As she made her way to the bedroom, she heard Johnson's concerned voice.

"Stella, it's your dad."

Stella feigned worry.

"Your mother is in the hospital," Johnson completed.

"Oh no, not again."

"I'll go with you," he got up and stretched his hand to get the shirt he'd just taken off.

Stella staggered to a halt and then stammered. "Don't worry. I'm sure it's just routine."

Johnson had already gone to get his jacket.

"JT, calm down. My dad is there. I'll be fine."

He hesitated. "Are you sure?"

Stella nodded.

"I'll get you a cab," he murmured and returned to the living room and rummaged for his phone.

Stella nodded again.

"Can I use your phone? Mine fell in."

"Again?" he asked, eyeing her suspiciously.

"Again," she nodded in acknowledgment.

Not long after she left, Kelechi locked the door and left the key in the keyhole then moved the coat hanger to block the view of the keyhole just like she'd done before. She went into the sitting room clad, only in a small towel. Johnson was washing the dishes. She took a plate off him and bent down to take a few drumsticks.

Johnson only had to see her in a towel to be curious enough to look back. The towel was covering nothing he needed to see. He cooed, "Nwunye'm."

Kelechi smiled and continued to select the

chicken she wanted, slowly.

Johnson held her waist. Smiling mischievously, she feigned escape as they sauntered out of the kitchen.

CHAPTER 16

A week had passed by quickly. Stella seemed to be on holiday as she went nowhere, her friends didn't visit either. Kelechi subjected herself to the pleasure of the voices at the other end of her phone. She'd grown annoyed, desperate, and quite irritable that when Stella finally left for Dubai the following week, she didn't talk to Johnson. She'd been so carried away by her feelings that she forgot to call Father Jude as she'd promised herself. Luck of someone to talk to came from a call she wasn't expecting. It was Igoni. She had mentioned stepping out to top-up to him, and he credited it before she had a chance to step out of the house.

She took a stroll when she felt the soothing breeze and gentle sun. Whilst walking, she called Father Jude. They talked for a long time so that when he asked the last time she went for the sacrament of reconciliation, she ended up making confessions over the phone. Quite relieved, after receiving absolution and a short penance that she decided she was going to surprise her husband, whose team was given some time off.

Stella was away in Dubai with her friends. What more could she ask for? She was going to make him *agidi* and *moimoi*. She'd overheard him tell his mother that he missed it (before he saw the pictures and letters). She picked up the money that Father Jude had sent her months ago, stopped by the bank to pay the rent, which was two weeks overdue, paid an advance of three months, and then stopped by a shop for groceries.

Humming, she took the items to the kitchen, washed and soaked the beans then made her way to the bedroom, almost dancing with the receipt. She opened the door and froze; her husband was making out with Stella on the bed that they shared that morning.

"Oh my god!" Kelechi exclaimed, shocked that they were making out on the bed, annoyed that Stella hadn't travelled and a mix of other reactions.

Stella seemed prepared this time; she wrapped her arms and legs around Johnson and didn't stop until she was satisfied. Johnson feigned disinterest for Kelechi's pleasure. Kelechi wanted to leave them but for some reason remained rooted to the spot.

"Oh, hi Chi, you should have knocked," Stella said and laughed haughtily.

"To get into my room?" Kelechi fumed and

moved menacingly towards Stella, but Johnson stood between them with a plea in his eyes.

"Your room?" Stella sniggered. "Am I missing something?"

Kelechi quickly showed Johnson the receipt while Stella bent down to pick her robe up.

"I'm so sorry," Johnson began to plead, reacting mostly to what he'd seen on the receipt.

"Johnson?" Stella demanded. "Would somebody please tell me what's going on?"

Kelechi gritted her teeth, her fists balled. "Please leave my room."

"Oh no, she didn't just say that to me. To us!" Stella cried in staccato, gesturing at her husband, who appeared aloof. Aghast, her mouth hung open, and almost immediately, she started swearing and cussing.

"Please, take it out of here," Kelechi snarled.

Johnson left the room and tried to tug Stella with him, but she deftly slipped away.

Stella raised her hand to slap Kelechi, but Kelechi was expecting it and caught her hand. "You try this again, I'll beat you to a pulp."

"Johnson, are you going to stand there and let her insult your wife so?"

Kelechi scoffed as she shut them out and locked the door. She tried to hold it in but unable to, picked a pillow, screamed into it, kicking her legs wildly.

“What do you want me to do?” Johnson asked, already bored with the conversation. “We’re broke, Stella. She’s been paying the rent for the past six months.”

“Six months? What happened to your salary?”

“Credit cards happened,” he retorted disdainfully.

Stella fell silent.

“You don’t tell me. The bank threatened to close my account, and then I registered for the online banking and behold, my wife has been swindling me.”

“JT, it’s not like that!”

“It’s never like that,” he mumbled and stalked to the kitchen, relieved that she’d bought his lies again.

“Are you taking sides with her? I’m your wife for God’s sake!”

Worry crossed his face briefly as he peered at her. He slanted his head, poured himself a glass of water, gulped it in one swallow, and sighed, “my wife would not abort my babies.”

Incensed, Stella shrieked. “You would take her word over your wife’s?”

Frustrated, Johnson shook his head. He wasn’t in the mood to let her sully his vibe further; he’d been looking forward to having unhampered access to Kelechi, but she’s messed it up by changing her flight time. "I believe you have a flight to catch." He trudged to the sofa bed and turned on the TV.

She took the remote control off him and cupped his face as she squatted in front of him. "JT, what's happening to us?"

"Now," he started, removed her hands from his face and dramatically added. "That's a question I want you to answer."

"It's not what you think, JT, I swear."

"Like I said, you've got a flight to catch." He was desperate to get rid of her. He knew it was a bad idea to have made out in the room, but he was sure that Kelechi wouldn't be back before they were done. He'd been so careful.

"Don't do this to us, honey. I can always book another flight –"

"You will?" he baited before he could stop himself and cringed.

"Well..." Stella looked down at her hand and pursed her lips.

Johnson sniggered somewhat glad that she didn't know that she had a tell - her response had given her away. He couldn't believe that she'd aborted a pregnancy. He retrieved the remote control and increased the TV's volume. "Have a safe trip."

The doorbell rang.

She hugged and kissed him.

Johnson didn't reciprocate immediately. He turned away to hide his tears. He had to admit; it had grown harder since Kelechi came back into his life to choose between them. He loved them in different ways for different reasons. They were strong, intelligent, and hardworking women in their right and their flaws unique to themselves.

Where Stella was feisty and openminded, Kelechi was diligent and reserved, and both women were loyal to a fault. He and Stella were matched intellectually, better exposed, but Kelechi was his downtime and uptime. Whether euphoric or depressive, he could count on Kelechi to cheer him, and though Stella could tolerate it, her tolerance was short-lived.

However, Kelechi knew that he was a cheater; Stella didn't. So, how would she take it? Would she be as determined as Kelechi was to look past it? Even if he was to choose Stella over Kelechi, he couldn't leave Kelechi emptyhanded.

Yet, he dreaded losing Kelechi.

The fog welcomed the hesitant sun. It felt like the sun, and the wind were having a mild dance as Kelechi stood at the door. Bored and hopeful, Kelechi decided to go to the shed. The landlord, in his note, wanted everything thrown away but told them they could keep anything they liked. The shed was a hot, dusty storage unit. It housed a lot of memorabilia. She smiled at the retro bookshelf. On it, she found a few dusty books.

Curiously, she touched them. They were covered with brocade, and the name Sarah stitched on the surface. She opened it and reprimanded herself as it was a diary and, therefore, private. She nudged them into a wicker basket. While she was taking things out of the storage unit, people began to hover.

"May I help you with these?" A teenager asked.

"Yes, please," she said and hurried back inside to use the loo. By the time she'd returned, the boy had sold all the things she'd brought out and most of the things that were inside. "What are you doing?"

"Getting rid of the unwanted, that's what!"

Dismayed, she stared at him.

"I did good. Didn't I?" he asked, smiling sheepishly.

The books were safely tucked in the basket. She added a few more books by her favourite authors before murmuring to the people ransacking the goods inside the storage. When they didn't respond, she started chasing them with a gentle prod. Amidst the groaning, she pulled the boy back and snatched the money from his hand.

"Is this all of it?" she asked, not ready to count it until everyone was well away.

"Yes Ma'am. You're real nice, so I charge ten percent of every sale I've made." He nodded proudly. "I normally charge twenty-five percent."

She frowned at him, amused. She had only been away for close to thirty minutes.

She gave him one hundred pounds without checking the whole amount.

He counted it and cajoled.

"That's all you're getting," she replied in a stern voice.

Downcast, he muttered. "But I did a good job."

"Yes, you did. But I wasn't planning on selling them."

"Oh, I'm sorry, I really am," he pleaded, alarmed.

"It's okay. Why are you not in school today?"

"Inset day."

"What's that?"

"A day for teachers," he muttered with a shrug as he rocked himself on the spot.

"I see." She didn't, but it made her feel foolish, not knowing what inset day was. "What are you doing in these parts?"

"My dad is the local fishmonger. I'm going to meet him."

"Oh, I see."

"You seem to see a lot."

"I do, don't I?" she chuckled. "You best be on your way then."

“Thanks Ma’am. Have a lovely day.”

“What’s your name?” she asked.

“Jayesh.”

“Thanks, Jayesh.”

She appraised a few paintings. Not wanting to risk selling them for less than their value, she took them into the house. She also took the flat-pack dining set, cooking pots that were as good as new. She gasped when she found a sewing machine and almost laughed when she found a box of haberdashery wrapped in a film. The former owner seemed to care about the sewing machine and the paintings more than anything else.

The hours that followed, she dusted, cleaned, and washed, casually admitting interference from curious shoppers. The sun cast a shine on her handiwork while she prepared to go shopping. As she heaved her shopping to the platform, the builders working on the neighbouring house came to assist her. She thanked them and quickly rushed inside to get changed, it would be dark soon, and the kitchen light wasn’t bright enough to cook in the night.

Kelechi walked into the room, her eyes on the mantelpiece. It hadn’t been there before she went to the market. To walk around the small table, she stepped back and squealed when she bumped into something. She tried to turn, but an arm held her close. Knowing it was her husband's, she bit her lip and reluctantly wiggled away.

"Nwunye'm oooo," he cheerfully murmured as he prevented her from leaving.

She shakily brushed the hair off her face. "What do you want?"

He smiled coyly. "Do you like it?"

Kelechi eyed him, suspiciously, "What?

He pointed at the mantlepiece, which was now over the fireplace. "You said it was useful, and after the effort you put in cleaning it..." he carelessly waved his hand, accidentally sprinkling dust in her eyes.

She squeaked.

"I'm so sorry," he stretched his hand to her, but she dodged it. He went after her but waited at the door and handed her the towel.

Kelechi mumbled her thanks. She slowly wiped her face. *With my biological clock ticking, is it wise to push him away?* All the activities of the day were supposed to help her fall asleep but did nothing to ease her nerves.

She kept tossing and turning and went to the kitchen to make herself a hot chocolate where she saw her husband. She decided to make one for him if only to say thank you for helping her with the mantlepiece and dining set. They barely talked to each other as they both held onto their pride, they didn't know they had, but to Kelechi, it was a bad idea to take away one's ability to say two simple words.

The following day, she counted the money Jayesh had raised and gasped. It was a year's rent and more. She had no intention of paying the next rent. No, she wanted to have a baby; they came heavy duty with financial consequences. She carefully wrapped it in her socks and tucked the socks in her shoes, just like her grandmother had taught her and laughed. It was a funny memory.

She nodded, reminding herself to learn to lean on those kinds of memories. She got up to ease herself and forced herself to fall back to sleep because it was still too early.

When she finally awoke, it was late in the afternoon. As she made her way into the kitchen, she noticed her husband on the settee with his hand over his head. There were papers on the floor, but the one in his hand fell to the ground as he gave into slumber.

Feeling cold, she assumed he was too and went to him to cover him. She had to hold her breath because of the smell of the throws. She moved them to the floor, went to the bedroom, returned with her duvet. She gulped as she covered him and cupped his face. He muttered in his sleep. Touched, she kissed his forehead, wishing she could stay angry at him.

She was tempted to read the letter, but the click of the letterbox distracted her. As she picked the letters up, she found one addressed to her. It was from her cousin. The letter she'd been expecting had arrived, but she was concerned about leaving her husband alone in his state. However, she was not one to break a promise, and it was only for a few days. She dished out some food and got ready to visit her cousin.

She left her husband a message on a sticky note and stuck it to his laptop before leaving for Cambridge and prayed that the few days away was enough time to come up with a few ideas of how to get past her predicament. Her future had seemed bleak until she decided to have a child. She had to prepare herself so that her children's future wouldn't be as bleak as hers. But most importantly, she needed something to furl her anger towards her husband so she could focus on her main agenda: conceiving.

CHAPTER 17

A knock on the door woke Johnson up. It seemed to have been going on for a while. He wasn't expecting anyone, but he used that opportunity to visit the toilet. He saw the bedroom door ajar and peered in. Kelechi was not in there. On his return, he frowned at the sticky note on his laptop, but didn't bother to read it. He turned towards the kitchen to quench his thirst. It was then that he assumed that it could be Kelechi and went to answer the door. He opened the door, not opening his eyes as he stumbled back to bed.

"You didn't leave with the key. Where did you go?" he asked.

"Hi!" Zainab drawled excitedly. Her eyes fell on his boxers - it was all he had on.

Johnson froze, his grogginess disappeared. He spun, his head slanted, on his brows a question.

"I'm Zainab. I'm looking for your wife. She was supposed to give me my dinnerware," she said hastily as she walked close to him towards the sitting room.

Johnson, not pausing, veered to the kitchen

when he heard the chime of the kettle. He wanted to ask if she wanted coffee and changed his mind. Being hospitable to a woman he didn't know was out of the question. Also, Kelechi admitted to Simisola being her only friend amongst women.

Kelechi would have tagged it, he thought. After a long search, he discovered that he'd been standing over it, a blue cellophane bag with 'Zainab' written on it.

Meanwhile, Zainab, not believing her luck when she saw Kelechi's note to her husband, scratched her head, contemplating. Doubtful and uneasy, she glanced around until her eyes fell on a semi-crumpled paper wedged to one side of the sofa bed. Curiosity outweighed caution as she bent down to retrieve it. She read it and gasped.

"This is an open door, a ticket, a gateway, *the* opportunity," she mumbled.

She rubbed her hands excitedly and went to secure the front door. Undressing, she made her way back to the living room. A quick message to her nanny and she discarded her undergarments, spread the duvet on the bed, and lay on it. After a brief survey, she tucked an arm under her breast, rested her head on the other, waiting in anticipation for Johnson.

Johnson changed his mind and brought in a tray

for her. He was oblivious to the change on the other side of the room until he looked in the direction of his computer. It was dark because the sun had gone out of sight. He turned on the light, blinked, and looked away.

Sighing, he thinned his lips, his brows furrowed; if he pulled her out, she could accuse him of sexual harassment or worse, rape. She was naked, so it would sell. He wouldn't be guilty of the sort, but the drama that came with it could add to his present jam.

He looked again and shuddered. Decidedly, he went to get Kelechi to kick her out. He knocked. Hearing nothing, he checked the bathroom. Now desperate, he went to knock on the door again and remembered that she wouldn't have left it unlocked if she was in.

Where on earth could she have gone?

"I'll get my laptop and lock myself in the bedroom," Johnson muttered to himself. Bracing himself, he moved to the sitting room.

Transfixed in the doorway, he tried to quell the bile that rose in his chest. Losing his balance, he leaned against the wall and held his head with his hand. He wasn't good at ignoring beauty when it came naked. *Kelechi is the reason I stopped womanising. Did she also have to be the reason I returned to it?*

Zainab roused herself and swung her legs

down, paused for a while, then moved closer and began to touch him.

Johnson frowned. "If this is a test... you're supposed to be my wife's friend."

"Come off it! What test? You're an attractive man, well hung. I'm surprised there are no fleas around. You must be a gentleman."

Johnson sniggered and stepped out of the sitting room to check the wardrobe. He returned, looking amused. "Did my wife put you up to this?"

Smiling, she tried to reach into his boxers. "Which of your wives?"

Johnson stuttered. "What?"

"What?" she drawled. "Do I look naïve to you? It was obvious on Christmas Day."

Johnson sighed and removed her hands from his boxers. "What do you want?"

Feeling sexy, Zainab raised an amused brow. "You're not naïve Johnson." It was the first time she'd undressed for a man since the surgeries on her breasts, stomach, and thighs.

"I'm married," he protested when she came too close and stepped back.

Johnson knew that Kelechi's abstinence from him these past few days had been a bad idea. He just wanted a clear head to come up with a plan. He still hadn't come up with a good one. Fortunately, he was no longer lagging at work. Maurice had been a bad influence then, and he was still suffering from the side effects of it. A mistake he was still making.

Was it really a mistake? He'd liked Stella from the minute he set eyes on her. She had taken his seat on the coach. She was grumpy and was wearing the university's cardigan, like all newbies. She was also spotting a hickey close to her collarbone and a pair of voluptuous breasts. It was then that he acknowledged his likeness for large breasts. Hers was epicurean, with nipples darting at him through her tight, flimsy t-shirt; it was hard not to stare. They didn't talk to each other then, but he had never stopped thinking about her. He had even dared to compare her to Kelechi more than once.

A few years after she'd won the competition that had brought her to his university, they'd started dating. "Coventry is a great place for a student and not a good place for job hunting," she'd said, which was why they'd chosen Burnt Oak after graduation.

Their choice was also by accident: they had each chosen random postcodes, and Stella accidentally dropped a squashed envelope in their cookie-tin dip. He was glad, for that accident kept them from living in the heart of London.

Gosh! Those bills would have fried my brain by now.

But Kelechi.

Kelechi was simple with such an uncanny honesty; it was scary. She had lied once in secondary school, and it hadn't gone well. Since then, she'd vowed to be honest. To keep that promise, she'd kept her life complication-free. But the Kelechi who came to see him in England was different. A determined, strong, and decisive woman. His concern was that she didn't confide in him anymore. She'd cry, clean her face, and all was fine. It was indeed scary.

And Stella?

It was evident that Stella was hiding something. He used to be so observant. Now he felt lost. Was it because there were two women in his life? Or because he wanted to keep them in his life? Or his bills? Whatever it was, his future was now scarier than a nightmare.

He was pulled out of his reverie when he felt something wet and sticky. He quickly shied away from Zainab, but she was fast. He wanted to control his erection in the toilet, but now she was blocking his path, forcing him to stare at her bosom. He bent down to pull up his boxers and muttered, "Kelechi!"

"She isn't in," Zainab sighed as she played with her nails. She sat on one end of the sofabed and slanted her head. "Lucky for us, eh!?"

Johnson sneered at her.

"You seem so distracted," Zainab purred, still

playing with her nails. "I'm good for you, you know. I come with no baggage or a long-term plan. Besides, I can tell you like what you see."

Johnson picked the duvet and wrapped it around his waist.

He saw the sticky note from earlier and peeled it. Groaning, he crumpled and tossed it across the room. *Kelechi, your timing is rubbish! Situations like this get complicated fast.*

Zainab watched the yellow paper hit the dinner table and fall to the ground. "What a swing! That force is one to reckon with."

"Leave my house!" Johnson snapped, his voice husky.

"Feisty is good. I need that. However, I have a proposition," she started.

Johnson quickly picked up his earpiece.

Zainab cussed under her breath. She had known it was a bad idea to leave the laptop beside the bed, but she wanted him to see the note too. She walked to it and disconnected the earpiece, took the laptop to the dinner table, and climbed the bed before he could get off it. "Hear me out!"

Johnson didn't want to. He was stuck; his eyes transfixed on the udder of the female requisite of a mammal standing in front of him. He groaned inwardly, his mind in disarray.

She moved closer until her breasts were a couple of inches from his face and stopped.

"You've got bills to pay. I've got money to give. Give me these two to three days. I'll make it worth your while."

Johnson gritted his teeth and cleared his throat and undid an imaginary tie as he struggled to avert his eyes.

She slowly pulled the duvet off him. "I saw your letter - a lot of debts. I could ease them. All you have to do is..." She tucked her hand in his boxers and smiled. "Please me."

Johnson closed his eyes this time. Her breasts softly bruised his cheeks. To stifle a groan, he cleared his throat noisily when she wiggled against him. He was steadily losing this battle.

Zainab caressed his chest as she straddled him.

Johnson gulped but said nothing. He was being assaulted, and he could do nothing to stop it. Not that he didn't have a choice.

Zainab sighed. "Just this once. I'll prove my worth, you'll see. Give me your account details. I'll send you the money right now."

Johnson thought of giving it to her. At this rate, she would have her way. It should count for something. However, Stella had access to his account, and Stella had a big mouth. What if Kelechi found out?

"I have five thousand pounds in my bag. You can have it for today's time." She tugged the rest of the duvet off him without resistance. "Oh, all these abs." She closed her eyes and relished the sternness of his manhood in her hands.

Johnson let go of his restraint and struggled to breathe. This might be worthwhile. Cash was always best in these situations, right?

She let go and went to her bag and returned a few seconds later with the money and dropped it near his hand on the duvet.

Johnson laid back and let her lead. He couldn't bring himself to watch as he'd just prostituted himself. Trying to keep Kelechi at bay, he started to chant in his thoughts: *It's for the money, you need the money.*

In the afternoon, three days later, Kelechi walked into the house and sneezed. The air in the house was stuffy. She saw Zainab, sitting across from her husband. He looked started. He was now wearing jogging bottoms but was still shirtless.

"Just the person I wanted to see. Please tell me how my food was," Zainab chirped, a little too eagerly.

Kelechi frowned. "I don't understand."

"I'm still learning to cook," she added.

"Oh, it was okay. Have you been here long?" Kelechi asked as she sauntered towards them.

"Nah, I just told your husband about the plates." Zainab lifted the blue cellophane bag for her to see.

Johnson eyed Zainab suspiciously when she winked at him. Kelechi caught that and smiled scathingly.

"Would you like me to offer you something?" Kelechi asked as she unhooked the weekend bag from her shoulder.

Zainab spoke as she roused. "Oh no, not at all. I've got a hospital appointment."

"Okay, let me drop these things in the room and walk you to your car." Kelechi went into the bedroom.

As soon as Kelechi left, Zainab grabbed Johnson's crotch and whispered. "I've taken down your number so we can discuss how I'll make payments." She rushed to the door on tiptoes and smiled at Kelechi as she approached.

Kelechi knew it wasn't an honest smile but wasn't bothered because they weren't friends.

As soon as they left, Johnson stuffed the duvet into the washing machine and opened the windows. He then returned to turn on the machine. He didn't realise that there were clothes in there from the day Kelechi left. He tidied as much as he could and gasped when he found a lace pantie stuck to the side of the sofa. Stella didn't wear lace and Kelechi didn't wear thongs, so he didn't need to guess whose it was. He ran to the bin, but it was empty. For the first time, he was annoyed that Kelechi was a tidy person.

He didn't realise Kelechi was back until she wrapped her arms around his waist.

"Wow, so jumpy," she said and turned to the fridge.

CHAPTER 18

I'm sorry, just so distracted," Johnson said, quickly as he curled his hand around the lace with his hand behind him. He turned to face his wife with a small smile.

"It will work out, you'll see," she murmured, assuring him.

Johnson raised a brow in surprise. He'd been careful. She seemed cheerful in an odd way. Perhaps she'd heard something, or Zainab had told her what had happened. Kelechi let go of him and opened the cupboard behind him.

Uncomfortable, he hesitantly asked. "Did you need my help with anything?"

Kelechi shook her head and continued rummaging through them.

"Erm... about your friend Zainab..." he paused, hoping she'd stop and turn to him when she didn't, he continued. "I know I don't have a right to choose your friends, but I don't like her."

"Neither do I." Kelechi shrugged. "But why?"

"Why what?" Johnson asked as he stepped out of the way of the tuber of yam she held.

"Why do you not like her? She has got big breasts."

"Come on, nawh!"

"What happened?" Kelechi asked, mid-slice of the yam.

"She tried..." he looked at his wife and held his breath as he fidgeted because she hadn't changed her stance, "to seduce me."

"Not surprised. Though, I'm surprised you resisted."

"What!?" he stuttered.

Kelechi shrugged.

"What do you mean by that?" he asked and stirred her.

"You didn't resist Stella, but you resisted Zainab. Is it because she is Hausa? Or because she has kids? Or because she is married? Which is it?"

"But she is your friend. I have got you. What more do I need?"

"What more indeed." Kelechi mocked and turned back to slicing the yam. She twisted her mouth in thought. "She isn't my friend but Simisola's. Only, Simisola's my friend, and I know I've told you this before. I had only three friends at Rivpoly. They were Simisola, Areta, and Igoni. Mmm, speaking of Igoni, I was supposed to call him."

"Why?" Johnson asked, moving closer.

"Because I told him I'd call as soon as I arrived

at Burnt Oak."

"Why does he need to know?"

Kelechi turned around, causing him to step back because she was pointing the knife at him as she spoke. "Do I tell you how to live your life?"

"But..."

"Don't even start! Anyway, I'm making yam porridge, do you want some?"

Startled and intrigued, he nodded. She was never unruly. There was always a first time for everything. He made a mental note to meet up with the 'Igoni' guy. He didn't need a bad influence on his wife's life. He left the kitchen and saw the money he'd forgotten to hide, tucked it under the laptop, and changed into decent clothes.

"Nwunye'm, I'm stepping out for a minute." He called to Kelechi and left the house with the money and two letters.

Relieved to be able to keep the landlord at bay for another two months without Kelechi's help, he hummed his way out of the bank. He was glad to come to a new arrangement concerning his overdraft. He returned a few hours later with a handful of shopping bags for Kelechi, a new duvet and some shoes for himself and hummed all the way home.

"Nwunye'm, I'm back o!" Johnson called out as he shrugged off the jacket only remembering then that he forgot to replace his jacket.

When she didn't answer, he went in search of her and found her fast asleep. He tore the pack the duvet came with. Spreading it over her brought back memories of the day he made her a woman.

He gazed adoringly at her and began to stroke her face. She was so innocuous. He feared she'd never understand the complexity of living in a foreign land and hoped he could protect her from it. He planted a kiss on her head and exited.

The wail of sirens woke Kelechi. For a moment, she thought it was by the window. She looked out, saw nothing, and proceeded to the sitting room where her husband stood by the window.

"What is going on?" she asked softly as she wrapped her arms around him and tried to blink away the sharp revolving lights of the emergency vehicles. There were two sets of emergency vehicles as an extra ambulance arrived. A lot of people stood behind the barricade staring at the scene, mostly filming it.

As her hands made its way down, Johnson arched his back.

"I hope they'll be alright." Kelechi sighed with concern.

"They'll be," he snorted as he cupped her hands, which were now in his boxers.

"I miss you," she murmured so lightly he almost missed it.

It was like his heart was a stone and had sunk. Her words brought the guilt of what he'd done with Zainab to mind, and he sniffed back the tears that welled in his eyes. He was glad the lights weren't on in the living room as he turned to face her.

"Honey, we'll be fine," Kelechi whispered as she wiped off his tears. "I'm here for you, always."

"It hurts to hurt you," he gushed - his sincerest words since she'd returned to him.

"Cheesy, but nice," she smiled, pulled his face to hers and gave him a sloppy kiss.

"I'm sorry for what I have been putting you through."

"It's okay, come here," she demanded.

Johnson sighed with relief. They hugged each other. He was getting alarmingly good at deceit. Perhaps he should be concerned. Maybe when he was done with paying his bills. Additionally, he seemed to have an insatiable desire for sex. It started long before Kelechi; he'd hoped it'd end with her.

"Have you eaten?" Kelechi asked suddenly.

"No, but I'm hungry." Johnson murmured into her hair.

"Okay," she retorted and broke free. "Let me make you something."

He pulled her back into his embrace. "Not that kind of hunger."

Kelechi giggled. "Naughty boy."

"It's your fault o! I don't know what you've done to me, but I like it."

"I'm glad you do," she said solemnly.

He cupped her face and looked at her a long time and quietly said. "I love you." As soon as the words were out of his mouth, he knew. It was the most honest words he'd ever said to her.

"I love you too," she said, more perfunctorily than sincere as she wasn't sure of her feelings anymore.

They kissed for a long time.

"Shall we?" Kelechi asked, stepping away from him and stretching a hand to him.

"Hmn, I'm liking this new you o!"

Kelechi smiled ruefully. She missed him, no doubt. But her intent was not just to satisfy her body but to fill a womb that craved evidence of breeding. Her visit to her cousin had proved useful. He'd suggested she starts taking folic acid and others too numerous to mention - the beauty of having a personal doctor.

No contraception. Now, a time to rime-and-grime her way to conception. Whoever said you couldn't enjoy yourself on the journey.

CHAPTER 19

The following day was quiet. Not so quiet, but she was now used to the shoppers et al. of Watling Avenue. The sound was somewhat soothing, like sitting on the sands of Buguma beach, listening to the waves lovingly smack the shore in the spontaneous dance of nature. She smiled as it rekindled a memory of the first time she'd visited it. It was the first and the last time she'd been there.

Igoni wanted to take her there, but she didn't want to sully what little memories she had of her husband. Igoni knew how to spoil a girl, and that he did with relish, but she loved her husband. Now she felt she could give Igoni a chance at proving himself. She wanted to have nothing hold her back by turning every stone. He'd invited her to join him to the premiere of The Wedding Party 2. Perhaps, she would start from there.

She heard her phone ring but wasn't so keen on being receptive or letting external thoughts or ideas disrupt her quiet time. She wanted to be overwhelmed with her thoughts until she could squash the unnecessary ones.

Nature's call was distracting enough to take her out of her reverie. She decided to find out who'd been calling. Igoni, Simisola, and Áyò. Frowning, she looked at Áyò's message first. The surprise came from the message Igoni had sent about a rain check. Not knowing what it meant, she assumed he would be unavailable for the following weekend as he had to be in the US.

Not keen on a visit from Simisola, much less Zainab and Áyò, she made excuses, and secretly hoped they'd stop trying. She watched TV, and during the adverts started, she'd weave in a bit of cleaning, tidying, and cooking.

She dozed off, woke up, took her bath, and while watching another movie, she dozed off again. When she woke up it was too dark to see; she had to grope around to turn on the TV and use it as an alternative light.

The newscaster said something that caused her to shudder. She didn't like the news channel or morning TV. At that moment, she couldn't take her eyes off the TV. She sighed in sorrow and bemoaned.

"The gun control malady is like a scavenging game used to breed opportunist terror. Why wouldn't a boy stroll into the school and shoot people when guns are easily accessible. Oh, look at the sixteen innocent bystanders who were making a future for themselves."

Shaking her head, she stretched her hand to change the channel and froze. Quickly, she rewound it to be sure that she heard it clearly.

A president of a country like the US suggesting that teachers carry gun? The world they live in is already hard, and the news always spoke of the worst of it – the very reason she didn't like it.

Johnson had heard her exclaim and rushed in. "Are you okay?"

Kelechi swivelled then steadied herself.

"Nwunye'm, what is it?" Johnson asked, wrapping his arms around her.

She closed her eyes to savour the moment. She was prepared to have kids. She took him to the room last night but couldn't open herself to him, so decided to give him oral sex. She had removed all obstacles as planned. She'd even increased her multivitamin intake. She seemed to be her obstacle and didn't understand why she was holding back.

Even now, savouring the nearness of his person, the hunger welling in her, her heart racing, she dreaded letting him in. She couldn't come up with an excuse fast enough to circumvent what was to be expected in the bedroom.

The doorbell chimed.

It took a lot of effort to conceal her relief. Luckily, it also distracted him, and while he went to answer the door, she contemplated her next course of action, a good enough reason to keep him at bay.

Johnson returned, wearing a curious look.

"What is it?" Kelechi asked absentmindedly. Her arms across her body as she idly played with her wedding band, which was now resting on her décolletage held up with sterling silver around her neck.

"You've got a parcel!"

Amusement twitched the corners of her lips.

Johnson nodded.

She shrugged. It was specially delivered and gift-wrapped.

Johnson handed it over but hovered. He felt an urgent need to know; to find out if it had anything to do with why she'd been lost in thought lately.

Kelechi opened it. First, she retrieved a large flat box and opened it to reveal arrays of chocolate balls. Under it lay cream chinaware with lids, moulded murals, and rosebuds. She removed them and saw a note. It read:

Your wish, my command.
You asked. You've received.

She lifted the final box, opened it, and began to giggle. Igoni had remembered. She tore the pack holding the dice and seed, quickly poured them on the surface of the board game.

Johnson frowned at her. He was baffled that she was excited about a Ludo game. He couldn't tell if she was excited about the person who sent it or just happy about receiving the gifts. He reprimanded himself for forgetting to give her something. He'd been too eager to be with her that he took a taxi home instead of stopping by Oxford Street to buy her chocolate as he'd planned.

"Who is Igoni?" he asked, trying to keep the edge off his voice.

"He's my best friend."

"He lives in England?"

"I told you last night that I was supposed to let him know that I'm in town, remember?"

"So, he lives in England," he reiterated.

"I'm not sure. I think he travels a lot," she said with a moan of pleasure as she bit in one of the chocolates balls.

Johnson decided that he hated this Igoni guy already as he was the only one entitled to make his wife feel this way.

"Would you like some?" Kelechi asked as she stretched the box towards him. "They are beautiful."

Johnson gritted his teeth. She knew he loved chocolate, but he wasn't going to have it because it came from someone he was beginning to loathe. More so, someone that was obviously distracting his wife, distracting her from focusing on him.

Kelechi, ignorant of his musing, came to sit beside him, pushing the box towards him. With a mouthful, she murmured, “Do try the one with green dusting.” Her voice was so sultry it was such a turn on.

Determined to win his wife back, he ate the one she’d suggested. He was going to make her look to him alone and no other. He pulled her onto his lap.

“Let’s play Ludo,” she said quickly and slid off him to get it.

“Okay,” he reluctantly agreed. It’s been only two days since his last encounter with Zainab. The woman who had now made him switch off his phone when he was home. She was useful, very useful. Perhaps he could manage to arrange a meeting. He looked at his wife’s eager face and worry crossed his face. Sighing, he shook his head as he tried to put his head in the game of Ludo.

CHAPTER 20

Stella returned a week after, and a week after her return, her friends came to visit her and were shocked to find the bedroom door locked.

"What new skeletons do you have in your bedroom?" Portia asked from the hallway.

"How do you mean?" Stella asked, pushing Barbara's shoed feet off the sofa.

"You locked your bedroom," Portia replied.

Stella eyed Portia suspiciously. "What do you want in the bedroom?"

"Your red dress," Portia said quickly. She was only interested in Johnson. She'd been in love with him since the day of registration when they crossed paths in the accommodation office. It was the only reason she'd tolerated her friendship with Stella. She knew Stella didn't love him. She'd used him to get back at Henry Hopkins for marrying Megan. A boss that's still dipping into another man's well.

Portia knew she was no better, but she'd never desecrate her matrimonial bed. She had bought Stella's favourite wine and hoped she was successful this time. She'd succeeded in causing Stella to spill her guts, but the problem was Johnson left the house just before. This time she hoped he'd be in to hear from the *horse*'s mouth.

"Someone's at the door," muttered Portia as she made her way back to the sitting room.

"I didn't hear the bell," Stella said and turned up the volume of the TV.

"I think it's your husband." Portia said and felt bile rise to her throat after she'd said 'husband'.

"It's too early to be him. I'll be right back. Don't change the channel." Stella mumbled and went to answer the door. She returned and took the glass of wine from Portia. "It was someone who missed their address."

Exactly two hours later, Johnson returned. Her friends made no effort to leave the house. They were still in the house when Kelechi returned. Johnson was the person who answered the door even before she inserted her key. He caught them hugging and would have fought with Igoni if Stella wasn't right behind him.

"Hi!" Stella said as she nudged Johnson out of her way.

"Hi!" Kelechi and Igoni chorused amidst chuckling at something Igoni said.

Johnson was rapping his fingers in his trousers. His patience gone, but caution stilled him.

Stella quickly wrapped her cardigan around her and stretched her hand out to Igoni. "I'm Stella."

"Igoni," Igoni retorted as they shook hands.

"Come in," Stella gestured.

"I'm sorry, but I have to catch up with someone. Rain check?"

Stella looking disappointed, shrugged. "Very well." She looked at Kelechi, and politely asked, "Had fun?"

Kelechi nodded and walked past her husband, smiling. She greeted the other ladies as she gaily walked to the kitchen and stored the takeaway in the fridge. As she poured herself a glass of juice, she took off her jacket. When she passed the ladies again, she hummed cheerfully.

Johnson gulped and cleared his throat noisily. Her dress was a chiffon micro-mini halter-neck dress with frilly edges. He'd not seen her leave, or he would have made her wear something less plunging, less provocative, less seductive.

Stella's friends stared at her, utterly astounded. Their curiosity came to a halt when they saw her unlock the door to the bedroom and go in. They looked at each other; another kind of curiosity was born, but none dared ask Stella. They saw it as a cue to leave. As they made their way out, one of them bumped into Johnson.

He didn't know her. At that moment, he didn't

feel like being polite, plus she was drunk.

"Shauna! Watch where you're going," Stella rebuked. "I'm sorry, honey."

Portia paused beside Johnson and took a long look at him. She didn't notice she'd been standing there a while until Pamela offered her her coat.

"Who is she?" Barbara asked Stella as soon as they stepped outside.

"A girl from home," Stella retorted with a yawned, trying to mimic Johnson.

"Woman," Pamela corrected as she exchanged coats with Barbara.

Eager Portia was now disappointed; Johnson was home on time, but Stella didn't touch any alcohol. It was stupid to be still pining over Johnson after all these years. More so, because he was smitten with *the* 'a girl from home'. Though helpless, she wasn't about to give him up.

"We know you've got a Ph.D. You don't need to rub it in," Shauna muttered under her breath.

"She is so curvy, which way does she swing?" Barbara asked dreamily.

"She is obviously straight!" Pamela said, rolling her eyes.

"Geez, girl, ease up." Barbara murmured and walked ahead of Pamela.

As they bundled into Shauna's car, Portia watched her friend for a while and looked away. Shutting everyone out in their banter, she closed her eyes and indulged in a fantasy of her union with Johnson. One day, she promised herself. One day, he'll be all hers. It was only a matter of time, and she'll be able to out Stella.

Stella watched the car drive off and was glad they'd finally gone. Her heart and her thoughts had been jumbled up for months now. It was almost the end of February, and she hadn't gotten promoted. Henry had promised. She needed the money, the bonus, the holidays. His assistant had told her that there were other contenders, but that Henry was on top of things. Her parents' mortgage was supposed to be a cinch. But she was in debt; her credit was hopeless. She had also placed Johnson in the same position.

Shauna had warned her to stop sucking up to her parents. Barbara accused her of trying to buy her parents' love. Maybe she was gullible because she was adopted. Either way, she had to be careful, especially as she couldn't afford to lose Johnson. She may not love him, at least not like she did Henry, but he kept her grounded.

She'd once told him she loved him, but that was because it was expected. Henry was the love of her life; he was the one she thought about when she made love to Johnson.

Johnson paced around the hallway. From time to

time, he'd stop at the bedroom door, poised to knock and freeze. He couldn't un-see his wife in another man's arms even though it was an innocent hug. Innocent or not, it was another man who wasn't family. He had to get rid of the *distraction.* He continued to pace and stopped when the doorbell chimed, knowing it would be Stella.

How could I let her enjoy the company of another man?

Stella's attempt at seducing him was now irritating him to the extent that he got off the bed and took a cold shower. When he finally came out, he paused at the doorway, staring at the bedroom door. The desire to shake some sense into his wife consumed him; the desire to keep their relationship secret hindered him. If only Stella had gone out with her friends.

He tossed and turned all night.

Stella watched him disparagingly, worried about his resistance to her touch. She had a suspicion that Johnson had seen or heard something about Henry Hopkins. His attitude had changed long before he accused her of aborting his baby and also when she didn't give him an explanation for disappearing on him. Portia should have kept her mouth shut about the 'Saturday job'. But she knew there was only so much she'd expect to get away with.

Henry should have been hers. There'd been together since their first year in university. Her relationship with Johnson started towards the end of her second year after she caught Henry with Megan. They'd fought and made up. She helped him with his coursework and almost got caught cheating when she switched answer booklets with him.

She didn't know she had it in her at the time, but she was screwing two men. Stella mused, smiling. It was fun being showered with gifts. Johnson had suspected she had a lot of admirers, and she couldn't bring herself to tell him it was all from one person.

It was during graduation that she noticed Megan by his side, displaying a beautiful engagement ring, but he'd promised it wasn't his. She didn't even know his father owned the company she got employed in months later or that he'd married Megan, with whom he'd cheated on her several times.

He'd given her the usual upper-class stint; "I married her because of her family name", and she was lower-class with overbearing parents.

She'd married Johnson a few weeks after she'd found out. Henry was so angry that he stopped her promotion. And even though they'd broken up close to a year before she married Johnson, she missed him and craved for him so much that on the day he returned from his honeymoon, they made out in his office.

She didn't regret it until she returned home to discover that Johnson had made a reservation at a very expensive hotel for Valentine's Day. The qualms of guilt made her stay away from Henry and requested a transfer, which only moved her up the ladder, bringing her closer to him. She was hooked on Henry Hopkins. He wanted her, before the start of work, at the close of work, in-between during lazy days in the office. It was sometimes hard to play her role in the house because she wanted to earn her stripes at work.

She also wanted her relationship with Johnson to work. Out of options, thoughts frayed, she mused over what needed protecting - her job, husband or boss. She had to make sure no one else in the office knew so that it didn't get to Megan - not that she cared much for the darned man snatcher. But until her parents' mortgage was paid off and her credit was great, her hands were ceremonially tied to Henry's supplications.

Kelechi wanted to cause her husband some discomfort. She hoped he got the message; he wasn't going to be let off easy. At the same time, she would get the much-needed distraction. Staring at the ceiling reminded her that Igoni was beginning to look like a pawn in her game.

Three nights out with him had revealed that she would never feel happy or complete with him. He seemed to know more girls than boys, and most of them were married women. The way they looked at him revealed that there was more between them. She could easily have ignored it, but with Igoni, it was a red flag.

She loved Igoni's company regardless of his flaws and didn't want to hurt him. She wasn't going to play her husband's game. She just needed to find a way to ease him away because she wanted them to remain friends.

Just before she fell asleep, she heard a knock on the door, she could hear a hushed sound by the door and a light rap but was too drowsy to leave the bed.

The following day, she woke up abruptly. Seeing the time, she decided to go for a walk. Nothing seemed to have changed around her, just herself. She shrugged and decided to pick up a few things from the grocers. It was going to be another mundane day; she could put it to good use by cooking.

While she was cooking, Johnson's colleagues arrived. Portia and Andi arrived simultaneously. They had no idea Stella had changed her mind about visiting her mother. They looked at each other but said nothing because another of Johnson's friends arrived at the nick of time and pressed the bell. They followed him in. Stella saw them and smiled.

"I was about to call you guys," she murmured as she hugged them in turn. "Why are you here?"

"I was made to bring you this," Portia said and handed her the file, her ready alibi.

"You know why I'm here." Barbara retorted coyly.

Stella shook her head, pulled her friend back, with a warning glare, and a stern voice said, "oh no, you don't. She's straight."

"Guys, the draught is coming in," Johnson called out, bringing their discussion to an abrupt end.

"Hi all!" Barbara cooed while Portia gestured her greeting.

"Welcome, ladies, Akhem here," he got up to greet the ladies and offered them his seat. He nudged his freckle-faced friend to offer up his seat, but he didn't budge. Barbara sauntered to the offered seat.

"You're so kind," she cooed as she gestured and sniggered playfully. "I'm Barbara. That's Portia, the shy one."

"My annoying friend is Nash, and that's Amos. Maurice is easing himself."

Portia walked to the dining table and pulled a chair. Just then, Maurice walked in and froze.

"Hi Maurice," Barbara said coolly.

"Hi!" Maurice cleared his throat so much that everyone started complaining except Barbara, who had only gone to the kitchen and returned with a cup of water. He eyed her suspiciously but took the water. She watched him drink the water and smiled when he finished it. She wiggled in between him and Akhem.

"Feeling better?" she asked with a thin smile.

He nodded, averting his gaze.

Akhem nodded his approval.

"The match will soon start."

"Oh no," Barbara moaned. "I hate football."

Portia and Stella rolled their eyes.

A few hours after the news was over, someone mentioned something about the news, and Stella didn't want to be left out because her friends had made a lot of contributions to the discussion.

"I thought Beast from the East was a music album," Stella stated as she placed a tray of Kelechi's cupcakes in front of their guests.

Kelechi tried to hold back the laughter that welled in her. It was a topic that had plagued the news for almost a week. She would have been clueless too if Stella and Johnson didn't always leave the TV on the news channel.

"That's true. It's the name of an album."

Maurice growled from where he sat, waiting for Johnson to discharge the ladies even though he was waiting to be introduced to Portia.

"So, what has it got to do with the news?" Portia asked.

Stella nudged Johnson for an answer.

"I don't know. I haven't really paid attention to the news." Johnson murmured; his eyes fixed on Kelechi as she came out of the kitchen. She was in a pair of jean shorts and a yellow vest that barely covered her torso.

"Chi, what is the Beast from the East?" Maurice baited.

Everyone's gaze was fixed on her, including the three men she'd never met, all good looking in their own right and they ogled her much to Johnson's chagrin.

Kelechi smiled. "Oh, how do I put it..." she frowned, tapping her cheek dramatically. "Well, it a term that the London Met used to describe what the weather would look like when the wind is blowing in from Scandinavia. It's a massive collection of cold air that accumulates that area from September until April." Kelechi paused. Sighing, she packed her hair in a bun and continued. "Hence the term 'Siberian High' and freezing rain because it's got a temperature, which is below zero and freezes as soon as it touches a surface."

Kelechi's phone began to ring. "Oh, they said there could be thunder snowstorm, so best listen for the amber alerts and stuff. Excuse me."

Everyone was dumbstruck.

"Who is that damsel?" Amos asked, getting up as soon as she was out of earshot.

"Amos, she is taken," Maurice said in a warning tone.

"No, she's not," Stella defiantly retorted. "She is just reserved."

Johnson gave Maurice a cursory stare.

Akhem raised a curious brow as he spoke. "Reserved as in betrothed, or reserved as in conservative in nature?"

Stella nodded.

"Which do you mean?" Akhem questioned, trying and almost failing to conceal his impatience.

"The latter," she nodded.

Johnson, already tense, couldn't warn Akhem with Stella being so close, and the evil eye he rendered went unnoticed. He was more uncomfortable than he cared to admit. Fortunately, the girls were playing scrabble at the dining table. Each of them distracted for varied reasons. Kelechi came back to the sitting room during the second half. She didn't know they were watching football because she had her earpiece in her ear the whole time until she slanted her head.

"Off-side!" Kelechi exclaimed, her eyes glued to the screen.

Everyone's attention was drawn back to her. Oblivious to their lingering eyes, she dallied watching the game.

Akhem walked quietly towards her and pulled her towards the chair. "Please, join us."

Kelechi followed, her eyes glued to the TV screen. She hadn't realised how much she missed watching football until then. She didn't care which team played. She found Akhem annoying but tolerated him. A few minutes to the end of the match, Akhem began to hit on her. She excused herself, went to the kitchen and back to the bedroom.

By this time, Stella and her friends had gone out.

"Wow, she fine," Akhem jabbed. "That would be a good addition to my deck."

"She is out of bounds!" Johnson snarled.

"Hey, because you're related doesn't mean she can't have a life, okay?"

Johnson laughed spitefully.

"Let it go!" Maurice warned.

"Guys, come on! She's an adult." Amos said and brought two six-packs, out of his knapsack.

"Boy, you bad!" Akhem jeered, patting Amos and helping himself to a bottle of beer.

Johnson was too angry to indulge. He decided

to take a walk. Seeing him get ready to go out was their cue. Maurice lingered.

Johnson lingered too and only left the house when Stella and her friends returned.

A few minutes later, Maurice tried to leave, but Barbara insisted that they leave together much to his disappointment.

CHAPTER 21

Roused by raised voices, Kelechi shook her head in irritation. Their constant bickering hadn't yet blended into the background, partly because she couldn't help listening in. This time, it was about an alarm, she involuntarily looked to the side of the bed to check the time. They were supposed to have left for a wedding. She reluctantly shoved the duvet, in a hurry to visit the toilet and staggered to a halt in the hallway

"You look like a pirate," Kelechi blurted out and grinned.

Johnson glared at her, while Stella nodded in agreement from behind her.

"I agree with her. Now, please take care of that noise."

"What noise?" Kelechi asked offhandedly.

"It's the alarm. The fucking thing knocked me down."

Kelechi chuckled.

Johnson shook his head disapprovingly.

"I'm glad you find it funny," Stella uttered disdainfully.

“I’m sorry,” Kelechi replied and let out an exaggerated sigh. “The alarm’s not mine. It’s not even from within these walls.”

“It’s fine,” Stella sighed as she nursed her arm. “I’m about to order Chinese, would you like some?”

“Of course,” Kelechi muttered half-heartedly. Following Igoni’s advice, she was to act indifferent, so sighing deeply, she joined them in the sitting room. However, seeing Stella’s legs on Johnson’s thighs caused her to lose her appetite. She managed to tolerate them until Stella began to stroke her husband. Angry, she got up, took the food to the kitchen, and dropped it into the bin.

When she returned, Stella was at one end of the sofa and Johnson at the other. Sensing the tension, she thanked Stella for the food and walked on.

Soaked in boredom, Kelechi distracted herself with a few too many phone calls.

Sunday turned out to be a lazy day for Kelechi. She woke up late; her body ached; she was sleep-deprived and in no mood to take her Saturday walks. It had been three weeks since she last spent time with her husband, the longest they’d been apart. She’d been tempted to leave the door open at night so he wouldn’t have to knock. But if she was going to win him back, she would have to make him work for it.

Unable to drift back to sleep, she counted the patterns in the décor of the ceiling. She listened in on Stella and Johnson and overheard her husband's discussion with Stella of how his boss wanted his employees to do a performance much like *Strictly Come Dancing* for his dying wife, who wanted a soiree. For their troubles, his boss wanted to award the winner three thousand pounds.

Stella wanted no part in it.

Anything Stella is unavailable for is an added opportunity. Kelechi thought and quickly turned to google to find out what the performance was about.

Soon after Stella left the house, he knocked on her door. She ignored it and threw the duvet over her head. She didn't know he'd entered the room until she felt something touch her. Surprised, she held her breath as her heart hitched.

"Nwunye'm," Johnson murmured softly.

She stretched and pulled the duvet down slightly.

"Nwunye'm."

"Yes, what is it?" she asked, stretching casually.

Smiling, he asked, "no good morning?"

She hissed.

"Hear me out, please," he pleaded as he pulled the duvet away from her face.

"Go ahead," she muttered. She let him then replaced it.

"Will you be my partner?"

She sniggered. He must not have known that she'd overheard Stella reject his request and wasn't pleased that he'd asked Stella first. She yearned for opportunities that'll put them together and alone. She missed him - she always did. She also hoped it wasn't because of inexperience, but she had no intention of making it easy.

"I will," she muttered and sat up.

"Oh, Nwunye'm, thank you so much." He tried to embrace her.

She brushed his arms off. "One thousand pounds."

"What?" he asked, confusion wrinkling his forehead.

"Did you think I will give you my time for free?"

Johnson chuckled nervously.

"What?" she asked indignantly, and she crossed her arms. "Do you need me to help you, or you don't?"

"I do," he paused and made an exaggerated gesture. "But I don't have a thousand pounds."

"How long will it last?"

Johnson eagerly answered. "Four months."

"That's four thousand pounds. I'll receive one thousand at the start of each month."

Alarmed, Johnson exclaimed. "Nwunye'm!"

She hissed and got off the bed. "Who is your 'Nwunye'm'?"

"Nwunye'm," Johnson blocked her path as he pleaded. "Let's discuss this nawh!"

She glared at him and clucked her tongue. He may not like parties or gatherings, but he was ambitious and was good at keeping up appearances.

It's a good thing she isn't super angry with me, Johnson thought. He sighed dismissively as he stepped out of the way for Kelechi and opened the door simultaneously. He could see Kelechi making sweat for it. He sniggered. He would have preferred going with Stella so he could study both women on an even kiln. Kelechi probably weighed more at the moment because he saw more of her.

Is it really possible to love two women at the same time? This question had a recurring theme, yet he didn't have an answer.

Maybe he was just greedy, especially as the two women had men trying to lead them astray: Stella's boss and this Igoni somebody.

He had suspected Stella of cheating, but the call from her father quelled that suspicion. Then he found the card for a women's health clinic just after he overheard Portia and Stella talk about abortion. He decided he was looking for an excuse to cover his cheating on Stella, or more like cheating on Kelechi as she happened to be his legal wife. If Stella was to find out, she would deal him the same coin if she was in a good mood or she would report him for bigamy.

The ridges on his forehead deepened with each mail and each letter he read. As he listed his expenses, he noticed a regular withdrawal and decided to investigate it because he hadn't used a taxi in months. To his surprise, it was quite frequent - two to three times a week, for twelve months. He was tempted to call his bank but he opted to speak to Stella first

Kelechi ignored him. There was nothing to contain his thoughts or bring it to focus. Determined to clear his head, he went to visit his colleague. On his way out, he stopped briefly at the door that stood between him and his wife and grimaced; the emotional door was still up. On the bus, he saw a young couple displaying their affection and angrily turned away.

His phone rang; it was his colleague calling to cancel. He remained on the bus until it got to its final stop. Whilst getting off the bus, a woman's tram got caught, and in helping her, he accidentally strung part of her dress to a screw. The screw unwound the dress. No one noticed except an old woman who pointed it out, but her fingers were knobbly; it seemed like she was gesturing to herself, and worse still, she wasn't speaking English.

A passer-by repeated what the old woman said with a shrug, but by then it was too late because half of the woman's dress was on the ground as a heap of tangled yarn. She was a disaster by then she was now wailing.

Who leaves their house without a cardigan at the start of spring? Johnson smirked dispassionately.

Feeling somewhat guilty, he ordered a taxi for her and hoped there was money in his account. As the taxi arrived, he made a u-turn to get the bus that would take him back home and saw Stella exit her boss' car and enter a waiting taxi. He shuddered and pulled his jacket around him. Something on the other side of the road caught his eyes. Unsure looked back, shook his head, and peered intently at the familiar car. He could see her boss because the car drove right by him as it accelerated.

On the bus, he scratched his head, troubled. "Was it sheer providence that his friend cancelled when he was already on the bus?" he muttered.

"Are you okay?" an elderly woman asked earnestly.

He didn't realise that he'd been gesturing and muttering to himself. Embarrassed, he shook his head. She nodded and handed him a copy of *Awake* magazine with a smile.

He smiled his thanks and turned to look at the window as everything swept by the moving bus.

CHAPTER 22

Kelechi looked at her reflection in the mirror and sighed. It was almost eight months, and she wasn't pregnant. She gasped into her hand, aggrieved at herself for forgetting to remove the contraceptive implant. She had unknowingly hampered her plans of getting pregnant and heading back to Nigeria. More determined to continue with it, she booked an appointment to take it out. She no longer saw the point in staying. Her husband cared a lot about Stella; even a fool could see that. She may be his wife, but she wasn't who came first. She could divorce him and maybe someday like Igoni enough to be his wife but sniggered in doubt.

She removed her clothes and entered the shower, and only remembered her towel after she was doused in water. Not wanting to run out of the bathroom naked, she used her husband's towel. Relieved to find him in the sitting room, she went to the room and slept, but a nightmare woke her.

She groaned mournfully; *my sleeping pattern has been a mess, now nightmares?* Yawning, she stretched and kissed her teeth then went about the routine of ironing and baking herself a small cake, but she didn't want to have to talk to her husband.

At that moment, the silence was priceless. She was tired of letting Johnson bring tears to her eyes. Husband or not, she didn't want excerpts of his time. She wanted all of it. It was her sole right, as his wife.

She groaned at her selfishness, but she wanted children, desperately. She'd heard of the pressure of late pregnancies. She also wanted to be involved in her children's activities and not just watch them grow. As if to further increase her frustration, she heard the sound of children returning from school passed by. Angrily, she made her way to the kitchen to shut the windows. Why did she have to be unlucky enough to live close to a primary school?

"Imagine how many children I could have had by now," she sighed and eagerly looked down at the passers-by. She smiled as she watched a mother debate with the daughter about the necessity of a Disney-themed birthday party.

She turned around and almost jumped out of her skin – she hadn't heard the kitchen door open.

"I'm sorry, I didn't mean to startle you."

Kelechi simply nodded, closing her eyes.

"Do you have any of your own?" Stella asked

curiously and almost hesitantly.

Kelechi raised a brow.

Stella gestured with her head as she took a glass from the drain, but Kelechi missed it. "I meant kids."

Kelechi shook her head and sighed.

Stella bit her lip and murmured. "I'm sorry."

"Don't be. It's not your fault."

Stella shrugged.

"I want kids too, you know, but your brother wouldn't let me."

Kelechi coughed. "My brother?" She twisted her mouth and averted her gaze. She'd forgotten about that fateful day.

"Well, you Nigerians are all so related that you find it easier to call each other that. Maurice said so."

"Mmm," Kelechi balled her hands. *Maurice!*

"You know Maurice, right?"

"Mh-huh," *Of course I do, the wolf in sheep's clothing*.

"I think he took a liking to you. He can be a bit too forward..." Stella faltered and gulped. "Excuse me."

Her exit from the kitchen was so fast that Kelechi knew something had happened between them. She knew Maurice was disgusting, but now she didn't have a name for what he was.

She looked out of the window again. Everyone

seemed to be bracing themselves from the cold, but that's because they had a destination. She didn't know where she was heading and hoped the passers-by knew how lucky they were to have a sense of direction. She didn't need to cook for her husband every day, not when he had another wife. Yet she took the soup out to thaw and turned on the oven.

He could always order food or get Stella to cook? Remembering her personal promise and her agenda, she mourned her existence and caved in. It would be her contribution to the household, she concluded. Besides, why would she want to deprive herself of what she loved doing?

Kelechi bit her lip as she thought about her finance. Perhaps it was time someone else paid the rent. If that happened, Stella could insist she leaves the bedroom.

They could just split the bill. She would have to find a convenient time to discuss it with her husband. She hissed, reprimanding herself. She would discuss it with Johnson. The ding of the microwave alongside the bubbling water removed her from her daydream and her phone began to ring.

"Hello?"

"You sound different on phone o. Very sexy, oh my gosh!" a male voice exclaimed from the other end of the phone.

Kelechi frowned. The voice was muffled. "Who is this?"

"Cool the pipes, na me, *babandbad.*"

"Igoni?"

"One and only," he chuckled.

"My brother, how you dey?"

"I dey as you left me nah. Wetin dey shele?"

"Nothing o. I just wan wakis."

"Na you dey reign. No forget sey if you eat alone you die alone."

"You don come o," she giggled.

"Now, that's my girl. I don begin think sey I go get to tickle you through the phone before you laugh."

Kelechi giggled again.

"Come and join me *nawh*!"

Kelechi sniggered.

"Chilax! I'm inviting you to join me for a movie premiere. *Okafor's Law*. We can go this weekend or next weekend, anyone you prefer."

"I don't know o."

"Your husband no go gree? I go tear shirt for' am o?"

"Husband?"

"I know sey na your husband carry you come UK. You and cold no relate at all."

Kelechi laughed. *That much is true, but I've been doing well so far*, she thought and sneezed.

"Bless you."

“Na you cause am,” she muttered pointedly. “Abeg, call me later.”

“Okay, your way pure. Chop finish. I’ll call you back in about an hour.”

Kelechi nodded and giggled once more as the line went dead.

She hurriedly ate her food and took her bath. She came out of the bathroom to see Stella was standing by the door looking in.

“How do you get to keep it so tidy? I like what you’ve done to the room,” Stella said with a small smile.

Kelechi smiled her thanks, frowned, and raised her brows, remembering. She’d added a wardrobe from the landlord’s stash, a few pictures, and a mirror framed with papier-mâché.

How could she forget the bed? The previous one was low and lopsided. She wasn’t a fan of white coloured wood but, the bed was high, quaint, and strong.

Stella smiled.

They were both smiling for different reasons. Then they sneezed in tandem. Looking at each other, they giggled just as Johnson walked into the house. Seeing them giggle, he frowned and prayed that neither woman had spilled the one secret he wanted to keep.

“Hi,” they chorused. He looked from Kelechi to Stella but was unable to read them.

"Hello," he drawled. "Kelechi, you asked for this?" he said and handed her a small bag with a pink label then turned to Stella. "You wouldn't believe who I saw today."

Kelechi nodded her thanks as she took the bag and walked into the room but didn't shut the door.

"Your boss, he literarily drove past me. He initially parked by the clock tower before he reversed.

Stella's glass fell to the ground.

Kelechi rushed out without thinking. "Are you okay?"

Stella nodded and bent down to pick the shards of glass. Her hands were shaking so much she cut herself.

Kelechi held her hand. "I'll clean this up go and take of that."

Stella nodded and walked toward the bathroom, morosely.

Johnson froze.

Up until that moment, it was suspicion. It had just turned into a nightmare right before his eyes. *Stella was the one her boss had dropped off. How long had it been going on? How was he supposed to deal with this? Her Saturdays had been with that bastard and not Portia as he'd assumed, as she'd led him to believe.*

He leaned on the wall for fear of falling and had started to slide down before stopping himself. He didn't want Kelechi to see him looking forlorn or helplessly sad over Stella, so he kept his composure. He exhaled deeply, stretched his hand to his jacket, and gingerly made his way out of the house.

Kelechi returned to find Stella hunched over, sobbing. She paused, unsure of what course of action to take. She gingerly made her way to Stella and sat beside her for a few seconds before wrapping her arms around her. Stella bawled, causing Kelechi to roll her eyes. She had to admit Johnson's behaviour lately was appalling.

How could he have left the house seeing Stella in this state? It's not like he hides to sleep with her.

Kelechi cringed, when droplets from Stella's nose, touched her clothes. She wasn't one to pry, but she was curious to know what Johnson had said to cause Stella's slippage. She tolerated Stella for a little longer and excused herself. She had only reached the hallway when Johnson returned. She opened her mouth, but he shushed her with a gesture. Relief washed over her, and she quickly exited.

Johnson tucked a foot between the door and its frame.

Kelechi looked at him with a frown as he hurriedly entered the room and locked the door.

"Can I spend the night with you?" he whispered

earnestly.

Kelechi crossed her arms dramatically and shook her head.

"Please, I wouldn't do anything."

Kelechi appraised him and gestured. She didn't believe him, but he came to bed, only discarding his jacket, shoes, socks, and shirt. She was both disappointed and relieved. Their hearts raced; none spoke for a long, tense moment, and then he pulled her into his arms. She didn't resist. After a few restless hours, they finally fell asleep.

She thought it funny that he had to wait until Stella had left for work before he could get ready for work. Kelechi practically ran into the bathroom to prepare for her appointment. Johnson rushed in with her. It was the first time they'd taken their bath together. It brought back pleasant memories that brought them to tears.

Kelechi felt uneasy when he asked her to scrub his back. She didn't ask for his help because she didn't need it though it didn't stop him from trying.

Kelechi didn't realise she'd been holding her breath until he left the bathroom. She hurriedly finished, left, got dressed. Being so distracted, she almost passed out when she found Stella in the house.

"Didn't mean to startle you, I've taken the day off," Stella started to explain and exhaled heavily.

"Did you, by any chance, see my husband before he left?"

Kelechi bit her lip as she shook her head as she pondered. *What is the point of adding insult to injury?*

Stella's shoulders fell again as she stalked toward the living room.

Kelechi, afraid that Stella would start crying again, took her jacket ready to make a quick exit. "I'm going to see the GP." Kelechi said, opening the door.

"See you in a bit," Stella said, a voice husky.

Kelechi scratched her head as she walked past the Burnt Oak library. *Why do I feel so guilty? It's not like anything happened between us last night or this morning. Besides, he is my husband!*

Kelechi bit her lip as the thought escaped.

He is your husband abi? So, why have you been resisting him? Initially, it was because you questioned his feelings for you. Now you want to see if you can control your feelings for him. It's you who's longing for him and resisting him still, and still, you who would end up with sleepless nights.

She heard her name on the intercom and looked up to frowning faces.

CHAPTER 23

Igoni was trying his best to keep Kelechi in high spirits. It worked because it kept her worries at bay, but it sometimes filtered in. She sighed as she looked down from the pier, watching the families and friends littered on the beach in a bid to steal as much sunshine as they could.

Who knows when the next warmth will be with Storm Emma still on the horizon?

"Kobo for your thoughts?" Igoni asked delightfully as he rested a hand on her shoulder and gave a cup of ice cream with the other.

Kelechi gave him a small smile and took the ice cream.

Igoni watched her lick her ice cream for a while.

"Do you think I'm making the right decision?" she asked, now watching the waves.

Igoni grimaced. Visiting Brighton was a good idea - he'd thought - but now he detested suggesting it. What was the point when the lady leading his heart paid him no heed.

"Igoni," she grumbled. "I asked a question nawh,"

Igoni sighed. "Honestly," he paused, shaking his head. "I don't know!"

"Don't take this the wrong way. I enjoy your company. It's just that it feels like I'm leading you on. I don't want you to feel like I'm using you, especially..."

Igoni cut in. "Stop! Stop, stop. We've had this discussion before. Besides, it was my idea, right?"

Kelechi nodded in agreement.

"Chi-babe, you're my star-shine. No other will take your place. I have to admit I'll take you off him in a heartbeat. But I can't, your heart is still there. I want you to do this. Let him yearn for you. A man must fight for his woman, *nawh*."

Kelechi looked at him kindly and smiled. "Is that what you're doing right now?"

Smiling, Igoni shrugged. "Let's take a walk, shall we?"

They walked for a long while.

"I've got something to tell you. I've meant to but, anyway, it's about Dumlesi, Baridakara's cousin," he stopped walking, forcing Kelechi to do the same. "I've been a fool, but there's no one I trust more."

Kelechi raised a brow. Her eyes twitching, she looked at the ground and then at the endless sea, trying to guess the length of the horizon as she waited for him to proceed.

Igoni let out a defeated sigh and began, "I have

a son with her. It wasn't planned, I swear. I went to the States to visit my cousin; I didn't even know they were married at the time. It just got out of hand. She swore she was on the pill. Well, years later, she calls to inform me that the kid was mine. After she had expediently divorced my cousin, she demanded that I take care of my responsibility. Of course, I ordered a DNA test... I've been taking care of the boy ever since. Please don't judge me; everyone in my family already does. I've never slept with a married woman. The thought has never crossed my mind until I met you again."

Kelechi blinked and continued walking.

Igoni stumbled forward. "You haven't said anything."

Kelechi laughed. "What did you want me to say?"

Surprised, Igoni stammered, "I... I don't know."

Kelechi shrugged and gestured. "I knew she had a child. I saw a picture of you and the baby."

"What!?" Igoni stuttered. "You knew all this while?"

"No. Just about two weeks ago. I didn't know it was yours until now."

"You're not shocked."

"Should I be? I was expecting you to have about twenty baby mamas, minimum."

"Chineke! My own no bad reach like that nah!"

Igoni griped.

Kelechi scowled playfully.

Igoni shook his head and pulled her close. "You know sey you fit kill pesin? Chai! You no talk anything."

"Igoni, I've always known women to be your weakness. I'm glad to know it excluded married women."

"Except you," he cut in.

"Including me!" she said in a warning tone then smiled. "I like the fact that you've always been honest."

She'd never liked the smell of salty water, but standing there on the pier, glancing down on the hundreds of people in all shapes and sizes reminded her she wasn't alone in the world. It was soothing in a way and resolved to know what the beach would feel like when it wasn't so crowded.

As they strode along the shore, they came across a heavily pregnant woman who made Igoni squeamish. Kelechi smiled, amused, and keen when the woman playfully smacked Igoni on the buttocks. She saw Igoni's pleading eyes and stifled a chuckle.

"Hi!" Kelechi said, smiling as she peered at the woman.

"Hello!" the woman's face was stern and courteous. "You're..."

"Chi-babe, his wife!" Kelechi said, extending

her hand.

The woman sniggered. "I see no wedding band."

Kelechi pulled the necklace out of her t-shirt.

The woman raised a questioning brow.

"It's now loose," Kelechi explained.

The woman slunk back as if she'd been struck. "How long?"

"Twelve years," Igoni murmured politely.

The woman's face turned crimson, then she nodded and scurried away as quickly as her legs could carry.

Igoni watched the woman go and sighed with relief. "I owe you one big time."

"What's the deal?" Kelechi asked, gesturing as she turned back to their walk.

"She saw me naked and has since pestered me."

Kelechi whistled and raised amused brows. "She saw you naked! Now, why does that not surprise me?"

"It's not what you think," he started and stopped, jerking his feet.

"You presume to know what I think?"

Finally, he brought something blackish out of his sandals. It was a crab. "I'm being serious here. It's not what you think."

"Okay o!" Kelechi raised her hands in surrender, her eyes on the crab, wondering for the first time why crabs walked sideways.

"Let me explain," he pleaded.

"Don't bother!"

"Abeg nah, make I explain," He continued.

Kelechi let out an exasperated sigh and gestured.

"I was her tenant when I started my Masters. I needed to save, so I fit get extra, you know. Na'im I collect one room for them house."

"Is she married?"

"Yes o! Her husband is in the same house. At night, she'll come to my room as there was no way to lock the door. I used to put a wedge. After a week, the wedge didn't work. No be pesin tell me to find new house o!"

Bemused, she observed Igoni.

"What?"

"You, see woman run, you? Wonders shall never end."

He chuckled and nudged her. "It begs the question of how well you know me."

Kelechi nodded, and they fell back into silence.

Johnson watched them with a frown. For the two weeks, he'd been tailing them, right after she introduced a man to him as a trainer. *What did she need a trainer for? Nothing! It was to spite him for getting married to another woman.*

He wasn't jealous. She was just naïve to think

that all men were equal or civil. Whether in Nigeria or the UK, white or black, it was the same blood that ferociously pumped harder when it saw a woman that could turn the heads of saints.

The annoying part was that she did it without effort and unaware. As they walked, others laying on the beach looked up at them, even those pretending to be reading. A woman with purple hair went as far as exaggerating their compatibility. He sniggered with disgust.

The audacity! The impetus! The man even has the temerity to place his hands on my wife's shoulder. After putting ideas in her head, he insists he doesn't know if she is doing the right thing?

Tired and hungry, Johnson didn't want to leave. He considered: if he stayed, Stella would begin to suspect his lateness and believe he was up to something. Besides, he had to return to work the following day with the project that he'd claimed was keeping him away. A project he hadn't even started.

Kelechi! Why are you torturing me so? Haven't I suffered enough? Why are women so impatient? A few more months and this sham of a marriage will end.

He grimaced as he thought of Stella, now sure she was cheating. After he'd announced what he'd seen, she became more careful with her activities.

Her phone was now switched off at home. She no longer came back late from work. He wondered if it had been wise to help her guard herself so. It would have been the easiest route to get a divorce; that way, he could come out clean.

He loved her, but he would never forgive her for cheating on him. If his suspicions were anything to go by, it would be that he had given her the opportunity to tidy up. He was scared and secretly hoped it was someone else. Stella could be viciously vindictive, especially when she felt caged or didn't get her way, but such was the way of women.

He also looked at his wife and his fiend. In his dictionary, this Igoni person was a stranger. Strangers were to stay out of his family's business. He had to do something about Kelechi's relationship with Igoni while trying to stifle any suspicion that may arise in his wait for Stella to slip.

Checking the time, he grimaced and quickly pulled on his shoes. The promise Kelechi had made pierced his reverie: "*I have now made my choice. To be beside my husband. To be a dutiful wife and mother to your unborn children. By God, not even you will stand in my way.*"

Yes. I will make it easier for you to keep your promise. I'll get her pregnant as soon as possible. I need to get this brain working. First, to get rid of that meddling stranger, and all will be well.

Someone tapped his shoulder on his way to the train station. He looked back and then down and blinked before looking away. It was Zainab.

"Hi!" Zainab drawled.

"Hello!" he mumbled, eager to put a distance between them and unable to.

"I've not seen or heard from you," Zainab started.

"Pardon me?" he asked, with an unwavering gaze.

Zainab flinched at his tone and slowly asked. "Is everything okay?"

Johnson wanted to pretend he didn't hear but changed his mind and asked. "Do I know you?"

Zainab, who was now being stared at, kept her distance from him.

Johnson hadn't realised he was holding his breath until he got onto the train. He suddenly didn't feel like sitting down even though most of the seats were unoccupied. He didn't see her again until he got off the train. He choked on gasping.

"Please, don't make a scene," Zainab pleaded quietly.

Johnson raised a brow at Zainab. He was upset at her for being in his face and reminding him of how low he could go. He didn't understand why she should still be running after him. *What excuse did she have chasing another woman's husband?*

Scratch it! What business did he have frolicking with another man's wife? It was bad enough that he stooped so low for money, but continuing was death itself, right?

He was exasperated at his wives too - Stella for cheating on him, her boss for sharing her with him, and Kelechi for being a loving, faithful woman.

Ever since Kelechi returned from seeing her cousin, he'd not desired any other woman.

Not Portia or Zainab and not even Stella, they were eyesores. Stella, whom he loved, he could no longer stand.

Was there an underlying factor? Something he may have forgotten to admit? Whatever it was, it had eaten into every fibre of his being and was creating unfathomable havoc to his mind, his body, and it wouldn't come as a surprise if it also affected his soul.

He'd almost forgotten that Zainab was tagging along until her phone started ringing. He closed his eyes, still walking as he tried to erase her from his side.

"Johnson, can we talk?" Zainab asked softly.

"No!" he crooned sternly.

Zainab glared at him. "Why not? Look at me when I'm talking to you."

Johnson turned to face her squarely. "Sorry?"

"Why have you been ignoring my calls?" she

asked indifferently.

He appraised her for a while and shook his head and had started walking away when she said something that made his blood curdle. "What did you say?"

Zainab defiantly raised her chin. "I'll tell Kelechi what happened between us when she was away."

"You will?" Johnson asked.

"Of course, unless... you know what I want."

He was irritated at her audacity, the fact that she defied him made him want to throttle her. "No one orders me around."

Zainab chuckled and flicked her hair, still defiant. "Well, there's always a first time."

"Then be my guest," he retorted with a sly smile.

"Now we're talking," she sauntered towards him.

Johnson dug his phone out and offered it to her, not unlocking it. Zainab frowned at his outstretched hand and then at his face.

"Call her," he urged.

"What?"

"Changed your mind already?" he asked coyly.

"We had a good thing going..."

Johnson came to a halt. "I don't know who you think you are. I don't want to know. You and I are never going to happen."

Frustrated, Zainab shoved him. "Stop, see, other guys are doing it. Even your friend Maurice."

"Now, why am I not surprised?" Johnson sniggered. He made a few furtive glances around and leaned forward, lowering his voice as he did. "I don't want to see you near my wife or me again. Or I'll call the police on you for harassment."

Whilst he spoke to her, he sent a part of their discussion to Kelechi as a pre-emptive measure and then played it for Zainab to hear.

Zainab was shocked. "But, that's not how it happened. You're vile, a beast..."

"Stay away," Johnson said coolly and briskly walked away. *One less problem in my spiralling world.* He slanted his head to see her walk back to the station; She had already crossed the barrier. He shook his head, not at all surprised that she would stalk him; He took a taxi home – it was the first time he didn't regret taking a black cab.

Sighing, He unlocked the door. It took him a few seconds to realise that there was something different about the house. The ambience, floral scent, aromatic smells, and the TV wasn't on. He felt like he had walked into his nightmare – of Kelechi and Igoni's interwoven bodies. His heart constricted in his chest. Squatting and cringing near the door, he rested his hands on his head, afraid to move further.

Kelechi! Please don't do this to me! Please!

He shook his head, reluctantly to go further.

It's not going to happen! I won't let it!

He immediately went to the bedroom door and turned the knob. It was locked. He knocked and briefly waited. He could hear soft music. Fearing the worst and not wanting to think of it, he headed for the kitchen to find something he could use to break the door.

He staggered when he saw Stella at the dining table. She was clad in a lingerie he'd never seen, and he knew then that she made the arrangement. A rush of relief, then doubt, then irritation, although intrigued by her effort, he knew what she wanted, but the thought of another man's hands on her was too much to tolerate. However, he needed something. Something that required he get his head in the game until he'd achieved it.

Let's face it, he thought. *You're using me, and I'm using you. Two can play this game.*

He went to her and pulled her into a hug before plastering her face with kisses. She sighed and hugged him tightly then jumped to wrap her legs around him.

"I missed you," he said coolly.

"I missed you too," she said, excitement and relief written on her face.

"I'm sorry. I've been distracted lately," Johnson murmured.

"Me too."

"Can I make it up to you?" he asked, planting more kisses on her face.

Stella demurely smiled. "Would you like to eat something first?"

He frowned, looking at the table, unsure of what was displayed apart from the oysters. He shrugged and sat down, wondering when she got the time to do all the cooking because she left the house before he did. As he sipped the wine, he saw the time and knew he had to speed up the process. He didn't want Kelechi to catch him at it, again. Not while he was trying to woo her back into his arms.

"Not hungry?" Stella asked briskly.

Johnson winked at her and roused. "We can always come back to this."

"By all means," she chuckled.

"And with all pleasure," he mumbled. He was keeping up appearances, and so was she. The problem was he didn't know why she needed to. Was Kelechi doing the same thing?

This was a call to duty that he had no choice but to fulfil. With that, he smothered his wandering thoughts to keep his head in what he was doing.

Stella giggled and sauntered to him, going down on her knees. He shook his head as he roused then carried her to bed, which she had already splayed with flowers. His eyes caught something at one end of the sofa bed.

When she was fast asleep, he took a peek at it and almost laughed out loud. She'd paid a hundred and fifty pounds for the set-up. He sniggered and shook his head.

Stella always went head-first in extravagancy, which made him worry about her. Everything had to have a designer label, even her undergarments. She had to take her parents, and sometimes their children, on holiday, twice a year. It was tiresome. Her pampering her parents was endearing as was suffocating that he'd decided she shouldn't contribute to the household anymore, but it was like presenting a snake with a rat. Now, he wondered how she was going to cope when he divorced her.

Remembering Kelechi, he cleaned up the rose petals he'd brushed off the bed and any semblance to a romantic date. Unsure of how to dispose of the rose petals and desiring the complete absence of it, he flushed them down the toilet. He glanced at the time when he was done, but it didn't seem to move any faster. He decided to work while he waited but was too restless to concentrate.

Hours later, just after eleven o'clock, Stella woke up just as Kelechi started fidgeting with the locks. Stella, seeing her husband hunched over the dining table, pulled on his t-shirt and went to get the door. As they exchanged pleasantries, Igoni couldn't help looking at the end of the shirt, which barely covered her privates. Kelechi noticed and tried to keep the sting out of her voice when she reprimanded him and watched Stella return to bed before closing the door.

Curiously, she strolled towards the kitchen and stopped at the doorway of the sitting room. The fact that Johnson was working gave her a sense of comfort. She knew it was selfish to expect him to do nothing with Stella, but she wanted some sense of belonging – of his belonging to her alone even when he couldn't be with her.

She went to bed: her heart, longing for her husband; her body, yearning for his touch; and her head, in hope for Igoni. She tried to picture herself in bed with Igoni and nearly puked. It was all she needed to know that she could never have that kind of intimacy with him.

Could I have it with my trainer?

Her face wrinkled as she scoffed.

He isn't even my type!

She scoffed again.

Do I have a type?

She exhaled deeply, massaged her abdomen, and sighed.

My greatest desire! Have my very own mini-mes running around. Would I be using my husband, knowing he isn't ready?

She reprimanded herself; she had exams in May, in two months. She couldn't afford to take man troubles into the exam hall. She felt a chill in the air and abandoned her thoughts to find the source of the draught then leaned on the headboard, looking out of the window. She watched in awe at her first snowfall, pristine white and glitzy against the dim light, which gave it a vague neon colour. Wrinkling her nose, she listened to Stella snore and pondered.

When does this marriage of theirs end? Was it not supposed to have ended months ago?

CHAPTER 24

By Tuesday, there was no sign that it had ever snowed. The Beast of the East snow cast had passed. Storm Emma had passed. The only thing of interest to Kelechi in those events was the unveiling of a forest that existed seven thousand years ago.

That Storm Emma did really count for something, how quaint! Imagine! The generations of that time, did they worry about school or political correctness, or even bigamy?

"They definitely ate at the time," she muttered to her rumbling stomach.

With that, she slid off the dining chair and bent over to place a marker on the textbook. Just then, someone knocked on the door. Not expecting anyone, she ignored it. When it became persistent, she briskly went and yanked the door open, and instantly regretted her action. It was Maurice. She tried to close the door, but he'd put his foot in and groaned when it struck his shin.

"There's no one to save you o," he said and forcefully shoved the door back, but she deftly escaped its approach. He used that opportunity to step in and shut the door behind them.

"Finally, I'll do what you husband couldn't do. I'll make you a woman and satisfy your curiosity."

She rushed to the bedroom, but he got there before her.

Kelechi's eyes darted everywhere for something she could use to defend herself - they were out of reach. He turned her wrists. In a blink, her hands were trapped behind her. He put his full weight on her as he shoved her onto the sofa bed.

Kelechi stared at him, dazed, her mind blank. A knock on the door unscrambled her brain, and she began to scream. He tried to cover her mouth, but she'd had tilted her head. The knocking intensified. In trying to shut her up, he grabbed her by the throat. She tried to shake him off, but his grip tightened. Feeling drained, she stopped fighting.

A while later, there was a loud crashing sound, and the door opened.

An Asian man stepped aside, just as two police officers stumbled forward. It was only when they had unhooked Maurice's hands that she vaguely saw uniformed men. They wrestled Maurice to the ground and alighted when he was safely in handcuffs. One of them moved to check her pulse. Asking her questions, she couldn't answer because, for some reason, words wouldn't come out. She frowned, thinking it was supposed to be obvious to them. Their words made no sense except the one of the ambulance coming. The Asian man hesitantly looked at her. To every question he was asked about her, he shook his head. Someone in red hurried into the house. It was a familiar silhouette, but she couldn't figure out who it was.

Zainab looked around eagerly for Johnson though a little disappointed to see the men doting on Kelechi.

"Ma'am, how may we assist you?" someone asked from behind her.

Zainab began to smile and froze when she saw a female police officer. Frowning, she looked back at Kelechi with a new sensation. A sensation that came from having a wrong impression of a situation.

"Do you know her?"

Zainab gulped and slowly nodded with a frown. She wasn't even supposed to be here or anywhere in London.

The woman brought out a memo pad and a pen. "Friend or relative?"

Zainab gestured with her head and hands.

"Are you a friend or relative?" The

policewoman repeated.

Zainab shook her head.

The policewoman frowned. “What is your relationship with this lady?”

“She is friends with my best friend.”

The policewoman nodded. As if remembering something, she asked as she gestured to the room. “What’s your name Ma’am?”

Zainab assumed there was more when the paramedics walked through the corridor to the sitting room; she looked on and absentmindedly muttered.

“She is Johnson’s wife,” Zainab murmured distractedly.

“She is what?” exclaimed Portia and Stella, who’d just walked in.

“Stel, she is joking. She can’t be serious?” Portia asked, her hand rising to her throat.

The policewoman was startled, amused, and somewhat annoyed. “Who let these women in?”

The returning policeman caught Stella as she fell back. Sighing, he called out. “A little help here?”

“Where are they?”

“If you mean the ambulance, it just left,” Zainab retorted, gesturing.

The woman sighed, forgetting her English accent. “Go, bring me water jó?”

Portia, now pale, blinked. She turned to

Zainab, who was already calling an ambulance.

The policeman who'd cut Stella's fall looked at his partner, surprised, but his partner shrugged.

"Are you related to that lady?" The policewoman finally asked.

"No, thank you," Zainab retorted, shaking her head vehemently.

"I wasn't asking you," the policewoman rebuked.

"She is my friend and colleague," Portia murmured.

The policewoman continued with the questions to which Portia half-heartedly answered.

Soon after the police left, the Asian man - whom they discovered was the landlord - fixed the door. Portia and Zainab remained in the house until evening. Portia restlessly checked the time on her wrist with a look of despair. Portia made her way to the door, then returned to pick up her folder. She got a CD from her bag to give Zainab but changed her mind. Finally, she stumbled out of the house, disappointed and fighting back the tears when she almost bumped into Johnson at the stairs.

Zainab made herself comfortable with two cupcakes and the TV. Zainab was already undressing when she heard the door and quickly turned her back to Portia and zipped up her dress. When Portia left again, she went to the peephole to watch. Now sure that Portia wasn't coming back, she undressed and lay on the bed, bidding her time.

"Are you okay?" Johnson asked, distracted and concerned.

"Mm-huh," Portia mumbled and burst into tears.

"Geez girl, what is it?" Johnson asked, pulling her to a stop.

Portia sighed, though she continued to sob. Sighing, she untangled herself from his grip.

"I don't see the point of doing this anymore," she said, looking for the CD. "But you can have this. Your wives are in the hospital."

Taken aback, Johnson squeaked. "What?"

"I forgot to ask which one they were taken to," Portia murmured with a shrug and quickly walked around him.

He ran after her. "Portia, please! Tell me, what happened?"

Portia briefly held her breath. "I don't know much. When we got here, the police were in your house, then we saw a stretcher being taken out. I didn't get to see who it was. When we got inside," she abruptly stopped to inhale, "we overheard someone tell the policewoman that the other lady in your house was your wife." She wiped her face with the back of her hand and shrugged. "Stella passed out."

"When?" Johnson asked, offering her his handkerchief.

She ignored it and dug into her bag for a napkin instead, then frowned in thought. "I don't know! Hours ago." She blew her nose and continued in her pursuit for the exit.

Johnson tarried at the stairs, unsure of going back to his house. He scratched his head. Desperate, his mind too jumbled up to be of use, he grimaced and walked quickly and quietly into his house, not bothering to turn on the light until he got into the bathroom. He wiped the beads of sweat from his forehead, then began to peel off his clothes, and at the same time, tried to remove an invisible noose.

I should have gone back home like most people.

He shook his head.

I have five months before my Visa expires. This situation will become a hindrance to its renewal.

He scratched his head.

I'm going to need a lawyer, a good one because I know how vindictive Stella can be. Why did it have to happen now that the government was clamping down on sham marriages? I don't even have money for a lawyer. Maybe I shouldn't have been harsh to Zainab. She would have been useful now. My next salary was supposed to be my mother's hospital bills. It's only three months into 2018, and I'm already in a ditch that's about to swallow me.

He was now sweating profusely that he'd begun to itch. Unable to bear it any longer, he decided to turn the shower on. A few minutes later, he went to bed, not bothering to dry himself up. He scratched his head as if it could help untangle his mind's distorted-maze-of-botheration.

I can't afford to stay in this house lest the police catch up with me. Yet, where will I go? There is no way I'm going to prison. How am I going to tell Kelechi? Where is she? I don't even know where her cousin lives. Was she the one on the stretcher? Who could I ask?

CHAPTER 25

There was a depressed silence; the cars on the street made dull sounds from time to time. In a way, he was relieved; he was tired of the pretence. With relief did come worry, the worry of what his future would be. He wondered if he could run away, but he couldn't even afford a flight ticket.

He felt someone beside him. He stretched to turn the light on but was pushed back. The warm body on top of him distracted him briefly. Not needing to guess who it was, he willing laid back; glad that one of his needs would be met and hoped she wouldn't turn on the light to spare him his pride.

When they were done, he said, "Stella, please turn on the light. I can't seem to find my phone."

Zainab stiffened.

"Please!"

Zainab hesitated and slowly got off the bed and stood by the door.

Sighing, he got off the bed to get the switch. "Fine, I'll get it."

Zainab quickly ran towards the dining table

and picked something up.

Johnson switched the light on. Feigning shock, he started, "You?"

Zainab shuddered and pleaded as she opened her purse. "Calm down. Please calm down. I have the money, I swear."

"What are you doing in my house?"

"I heard what happened! I came as quickly as I could," she stretched out a shaky hand with the wad of notes towards him. "I brought this, as usual."

Feeling slighted, he snapped. "That does not answer my question."

"Please forget the questions *nawh*! I've been waiting. I've stayed out of your way, as you requested."

"Requested?"

Zainab winced. "I brought more." She dug into her purse and produced another bundle. "Two thousand pounds. It's all I've got. Today's Friday, just for the weekend. I'll not bother you anymore."

He sniggered and began to walk away.

"Okay, I'll pay more," she looked at him eagerly. "Just tell me the account number to send it to."

It was all Johnson needed to hear. He slanted his head, smiling in his mind. Following his gaze, Zainab cautiously walked to the hallway, where she found his wallet on the floor on top of his trouser and turned her attention back to him, but he was no longer standing there. When he returned from the kitchen, she showed him his card and her account, to which he expertly dramatized his reluctance. Zainab, happy that he was coming around and not wanting to give him a chance to change his mind, pulled him towards the bedroom. He withdrew his hand and went back to the kitchen, then returned to the sofa bed. She waited a few minutes, then came back to join him.

The following day, he looked at the phone and frowned, sure that he hadn't switched it to silent. He squinted at Zainab, who was curled up in sleep with her back turned to him. He'd received four text messages but decided the one from his landlord was most important.

A friend of yours had been arrested for attempted rape and GBH. The lady he attempted to rape is reported to be your wife; I'm disappointed in you, John.

You'll need a lawyer for bigamy if they (police) decide to pursue it. The affected lady was taken to Northwick Park Hospital.

Johnson would have left for the hospital right away but for fear of Kelechi discovering that he'd been with another woman. He stopped by the bank before heading to the hospital.

Kelechi didn't want to see him, so he went in search of Stella and discovered that she had been discharged the same day.

Johnson returned a few hours later, staggering into the house. He morosely peeled off his clothes and slid into bed. He understood Kelechi not desiring his presence, but he couldn't unsee her hand in Igoni's, and this image followed him all day, everywhere. Defeated and heartbroken, he barely noticed Zainab join him a few minutes later.

His plan had always included Kelechi until he met Stella. More than a year after Kelechi returned into his life, he hadn't ended it with Stella. He still couldn't decide which woman he cared about the most. He could absolutely relate to polygamous men. Maybe he could try to focus on the one he loved more, but which one? His feelings for both women weren't the same, but they ran high and deep.

Could it be Stella? She came from a different background, and though her understanding of love was warped, she was independently ambitious. He had to admit he wanted a woman of the same standing as his, which was part of the reason he'd chosen to marry Stella.

However, Kelechi's selfless determination and strength always made him weak at the knees. Kelechi was no doormat; she'd proven that on more than one occasion. He'd been aloof to anything concerning her, past and present and would never have known that she'd been studying at the University of Westminster if he hadn't overheard her discussions with Igoni. She would be sitting her exams soon, and he didn't even know. What kind of husband did that make him?

She was gradually slipping off his arms. He'd been so engrossed with keeping her a secret that he was about to lose her to another man. And that fear overwhelmed him more than anything else, even now. She could make a cave a castle – that much he always knew. What couldn't he have been satisfied with that?

But something seemed to pull him back to Stella. He had no excuse for marrying Stella. He's marrying her for papers was the excuse he'd given everyone. Stella got him, she fed his wild side, always - when she wasn't partying that is. The selfish part was that he didn't want to share her with her boss – the man he detested in university for the way he used girls. Funny how the tables have turned.

As he watched Zainab, he knew he'd have to let it all go. First, Zainab, as soon as it was midnight on Sunday; Sign the divorce papers to end things with Stella and then drag Kelechi back to Nigeria with him if possible. He needed to explain a few things to Kelechi. He hoped letting her know that no woman could take her place was enough.

He sighed and grimaced at the same time. His mind rattled with ideas, hopes, wishes, and a lot of what-ifs. The plan had been to relieve himself of Zainab at midnight the following day. But as the doctors wanted to keep Kelechi a few more days, he decided to keep his thoughts at bay with Zainab.

As he ejaculated, he wondered if he could let Stella go. He remembered the CD Portia had given him earlier and got off the bed leaving behind a disgruntled Zainab.

CHAPTER 26

Kelechi had looked away when her husband dropped in the day before. The moment she saw her hand in Igoni's, she wondered, *would I ever truly love you? Would I ever be able to get over my husband? Am I only angry at him? Could I ever forgive him? It was easy to preach, forgiveness, but you'd only know when you've been hurt, right?*

Her not wanting to see her husband was a half-hearted request. She would have gone after him if she wasn't so weak. She was still thinking of what she wanted and what she needed, yet unable to decide between the two. She'd considered divorce, but it went against everything she believed in. More so, in her heart of hearts, she knew, if she towed that path, she would never remarry.

She shook her head. It would be easier to forgive than forget because she could still hear Stella's passionate throes in her head, and she still couldn't un-see Stella on her husband. Mrs Barine had told her that it took her years to forget her husband's infidelity, but had forgotten to add the recipe of how she managed to get along with him or look past it. She couldn't even let Johnson touch her.

What if he is indeed in love with Stella? Would I feel different if Stella was out of the picture? Am I being selfish? I just can't ease into it! I want my husband to myself. What happened to my simple life? Oh God, help me! I've never been so confused.

Sighing, she withdrew her hand from Igoni's and turned her back to him, unable to hold back her tears. From her reflection, she could see Igoni looking helpless. She vowed then to end whatever it was they had. She had too much sympathy for him to want to be in a relationship with him.

Who can tolerate being second best? I know I can't. I may never stop loving my husband, but I will never use any man.

She exhaled and wiped her tears. She didn't care about what their excuse was for keeping her. She was going home as soon as she was strong enough. She would focus on her volunteering job and continue preparing for her exams. Hopefully, by the end of it, she would be able to come up with a plan.

Soon after she was discharged two days later, she hurried home; she wasn't ready to face her husband and made sure she returned early enough to be securely tucked in her hideaway. It was the first time she wasn't worried about using up her money on international calls, yet she made none. She couldn't afford to, not when she had her sanity to think of, especially with everyone asking after her husband.

For a long time, she'd enjoyed listening to the footfalls of passers-by on Watling Avenue, but now she was desperate to shut it all out. Her brain felt like it was about to implode from the penetrating racket on the street to the imploring monologue of her thoughts.

She'd been with her cousin only four days, and she was already done with it. Now here, she wanted to run away again. Two more days and she'd be running back, but how long did she want to keep passing through both houses?

She glanced at the calendar for the umpteenth time and sighed. She had only come to England to be with her husband, become a mother. To get to see her husband, she sold off all that she owned in Nigeria, which wasn't much. She wasn't getting any younger. It was like he'd married her to take care of his ailing parents, but looking after his parents was not her primary duty.

One fear continued to gnaw at her: fear of starting over. She always believed that a man cheated because his wife wasn't good enough in bed or had an inept cooking skill or didn't communicate with him. She didn't know if she was great at all these things, but she knew she was good and had given it her all. She never believed distance made the heart grow fonder, and her husband's action was further proof.

Why do I get to be the odd one?

CHAPTER 27

The day after she had returned from her cousin's house. She walked into Stella unpacking a few shopping bags into a suitcase. She hadn't expected anyone to be in and quickly snuck into the bathroom and closed her eyes, hoping the approaching footsteps weren't heading in her direction. It stopped and began to recede.

Portia chuckled, gesturing. "It's sweating!"

Stella looked up briefly. "What?"

"Come and see, your window, is it supposed to be doing that?"

Stella walked over to her friend's side. "Oh, you mean, condensation."

"Is that what it is? I would never have known."

"Portia, where is your head?" Stella asked after her friend's phone rang a second time.

"Mmm?" Portia asked absentmindedly.

"Your phone, if you don't want me to break it," Stella moaned.

"Easy, okay? I didn't know it was ringing." She scrolled through the phone and yelped. "I have to go." She bent down to retrieve her shoes from under the dining table.

"Already?"

"I forgot to hand in my report. Sorry, I really have to go," Portia retorted, blew her a kiss and left.

Kelechi sighed and tiptoed towards the bedroom.

"No need, I've already seen you," Stella murmured.

"I don't want to be involved," Kelechi started.

"You already are," Stella quipped with a wave of the hand.

Kelechi leaned on the wall near the hallway, unsure of what was expected of her.

Stella dumped the clothes and stood akimbo and asked. "Did you know? Was this game for both of you? A rush? Or something?"

Confused, Kelechi shook her head, frowning.

"I feel so stupid for not seeing what everyone else saw!"

Kelechi shrugged. She wasn't ready to discuss her husband but was curious to know what their new fight was about.

"Why would you let a man do this to you?"

Kelechi's frown deepened. *What happened while I was away?*

"When did you know?" Stella asked and plopped on the sofa, no longer a bed.

Kelechi noticed and blinked. It had always been

a sofa bed; it now made the room look sparse.

"This is not the way it is supposed to be. I was so angry, but I'm afraid I have nothing for you. I'm sapped."

Kelechi grimaced and sighed again. She had too much on her mind to understand how to react to Stella, and whatever was going on with her. Hearing the clink of keys, she turned to see Johnson walked in with a man she'd never met.

"Stella, we need to talk," Johnson said.

Kelechi curiously lingered.

"You wish you fraudster!" Stella shouted and tossed the clothes she was folding at him.

"Oh, get a grip. You've been playing me all along," Johnson retorted and hurled the clothes on the chair beside her.

"Did you even love me?" Stella asked. It sounded like a plea.

Johnson sniggered and winced.

The man he came with cleared his throat.

Johnson nodded at the man. "As I said, we need to talk."

Stella started crying. "You had a wife, you bastard. She was in my bedroom while I stayed on this sofa. After all, we've been through? JJ, did you ever love me?"

Kelechi froze. She wished she had followed her instinct and returned to her room.

Johnson shook his head. His shoulders bowed

in defeat.

"Answer me! You're quiet because that tramp is here?"

Probably? Kelechi wanted to know how he felt about Stella, but at the same time, she wanted to be invisible.

"Don't ever call her that!" Johnson snarled.

"Johnson!" the man with him warned.

Johnson telling Stella off washed away the sympathy welling in her for her co-wife. She wanted nothing more than to make love to him right then. She stifled the appetite for her husband's touch with a groan and began to leave the room quietly, but then her sandals gave her away.

"Oh no, you don't!" Stella ordered. "I want you to know the beast we married. You may have a hold on him, dearie, but wait! Wait, until you loosen that grip and this," she finally inhaled, gesturing wildly. "This is what he'll do to you."

"Has he not already done that?" Kelechi asked in a very low voice and sneered at Stella.

Johnson turned his back to the rest of them, his head low.

Kelechi raised a curious brow when she saw something remotely like relief cross Stella's face. It was quickly replaced by a blank expression. The smile was still there, the smile that twitched the sides of Stella's mouth, the colour that rose from her neck and the glint in her eyes. Yes, Stella was relieved and relishing the moment, but her shoulders also bore defeat. And that was what Kelechi was curious about, but not curious enough to ask.

Kelechi looked on. Suddenly exhausted, she left for her room.

Stella, feeling stung by Kelechi's reaction, retorted, "You know what? He loved doing it with me. Was he better than Henry? Of course not! He was a tool, an available tool. I got him the only way I could."

"That's enough!" Johnson thundered.

The man beside him hissed and put his phone back in his pocket, evidently annoyed at Johnson's interruption.

Kelechi, sitting at the edge of the bed, rolled her eyes and muttered to herself, "now he speaks?" She wanted to ease herself, but her dramatic exit restrained her.

Stella chuckled. "Why? You don't want her to know how it was with you?" She untied the belt, and the dress came apart. She was wearing nothing underneath, her breast silently giggled as she wiggled out of the dress.

Kelechi, unable to contend with her bladder any longer hurried out of the bedroom and froze. At the same time, the man with Johnson dropped his glass of water. No one reacted to the shattering glass, perhaps too shocked at Stella's effrontery to react. She blinked several times; her body refused to move even when Stella began to touch herself. She was intrigued by Stella's brazen arrogance, and somewhat envious - the one thing she wished she could be, *audacious and deliberate*.

"Our first time," Stella started, winked at Kelechi, and turned her gaze to Johnson.

Kelechi wanted to see Johnson's reaction, but her bladder pleaded desperately. She had held the urge to urinate for quite a while.

Stella moaned with her eyes closed and continued. "Remember? It was in the shower. You used to call it *the cold shower*. You were the first guy to go south. I parted my legs like so... and you moaned on your knees as you pleased me."

"I never did that!" Johnson started to defend himself and turned to plead with Kelechi, but she wasn't there. He could almost feel her wrinkle her face at him. Somehow, he felt ashamed, but then he had to defend himself.

"Oh, that's right! T'was Henry," Stella said thoughtfully, scratching her head and wrap her hair. "Or, was it Maurice?"

Johnson flexed his muscles and tightly closed his eyes.

"Any-who, he wasn't as enormous as my soon-to-be-defunct husband here, but he knew how to satisfy my cravings. He had this subtle way of nibbling at my nipples. Oh! It felt so nice when he blew the pain away. He'll caress and kiss my inner thighs like so until I'd beg him to take me. And then he'll bring me close to the edge and pause several times. Oh no, he was mean-spirited," Stella sighed and looked at Johnson dreamily. "He wasn't you. He was formidable. He still is, but he isn't you."

She was quiet for some time then exhaled dramatically. "It doesn't end there! He'll make me lay back on his desk and order me to bring myself to pleasure without touching my clitoris like so."

She moaned as she touched herself, closing her eyes until she climaxed; Johnson and the man never took their eyes off her.

She sighed and slowly put her dress back on. "I've always wanted to do that for you, but I'm doing this for me." Stella frowned and shrugged. "I guess."

Each man, embarrassed, shielded their crotch with what they had in their hands. Johnson's eyes searched for his other wife with curious worry, his first wife, that is.

CHAPTER 28

Kelechi had slipped away from the bathroom into the bedroom. She'd been trying to bring her libido back in check. Her privates were already throbbing, and she could tell that she'd wet her panties, but she didn't have a pinch of Stella's courage. Sex had been looming over her for a long time now. She didn't understand it. She needed an outlet if she couldn't reel in the desire that was setting in. She had already ended her relationship with Igoni, whatever it was.

Johnson stared at Stella's nipples, which peeked at him through her thin jersey dress where she casually rested and shook his head. He turned to the man beside him and shoved the man back to reality. The man scrambled for a while and produced a set of papers and approached Stella cautiously then dropped the papers beside her while resisting the urge to touch her.

Johnson began to pace impatiently, his eyes wandering towards the only bedroom in the house. He was so agitated that it was Igoni who'd caused Kelechi's phone to ring that he almost cried with relief when she responded in a clipped tone; there was always underlying laughter in her tone when she spoke with Igoni. He clenched his teeth. *If she chooses Igoni over me, it would be my fault. How will I be able to live with that?*

A few minutes later, he heard her unlock her door and hurried to the hallway. There, he saw her reach out for her jacket.

"Where are you going?" he asked, unable to hide his discomfort and walked towards her in a determined pace.

Kelechi slanted her head, a little amused and she scoffed.

He gulped. "Don't come back late," he said and added softly, "be safe."

Stella squinted at him and then at Kelechi. The other man seemed to have disappeared from the scene.

As soon as she left, Stella roused herself and undid the dress again. "Finally, the coast is clear. Now JJ, come to mama," Stella cooed and jumped over the settee then waltzed toward him. "We know you want me."

The man returned and frowned when he noticed that the papers were untouched. "You need to sign these papers, ma'am."

Stella's smile widened. "A lawyer! I would

never have guess," she muttered as she appraised the man. "You want me to sign those papers just as much as I want to keep you."

"What do you want, ma'am?" the lawyer asked calmly and tucked his hands in his pocket.

Stella pointed at Johnson and beckoned him.

Johnson frowned at the lawyer. He had no intention of offering Stella anything. If anything, he'd like her to pay him all she owed him. But if she didn't sign the paper, she may as well have buried him. The lawyer was uncomfortable with his idea, but if it worked, then it worked.

"JJ here knows what I want," she said, not taking her eyes off him. "All this fuss to prove your love to that girl. Such passion. Is she a virgin? Men are obsessed with such things. I wonder why?" she sighed. She was now standing nose to nose with Johnson.

Johnson didn't move. His hands curled into fists in his trouser pockets in his effort to resist checking the door. He wanted to rip the clothes of Stella and make her recant what she'd said about her boss. Still, he couldn't afford to let Kelechi catch him again, not with Igoni in the picture. If she touched herself to taunt him, what would she do if she noticed that he was paying more attention to Kelechi. He wanted so much to relieve himself of the tension she'd caused him but had no intention of giving her the satisfaction of winning.

Stella sauntered to him then turned her back to him. She gave his groin a massage with her buttocks then turned around to caress him, working her way down to the belt of his trousers.

Johnson gritted his teeth and quickly flicked her hands away.

She shrugged and went to lay on the sofa. “Make mama cry for mercy, and I’ll give you your heart’s desire. You know you want to. Why torture yourself so?”

“In your dreams,” Johnson snorted, realising that he’d been holding his breath. He wanted her desperately. Yet he didn’t want to kiss his chances with Kelechi goodbye. Perhaps he should have asked her where she was going so he would be able to gauge how long she’d be away.

“Well, that’s my offer,” Stella said matter-of-factly and began to play with her hair.

“And you’ll get not-” Johnson stopped himself and frowned. He looked at his fists and unfolded his hands, already sweating and trying with difficulty to level his breathing.

“How about everyone calms down,” the lawyer returned, casting a pitiful glance at his client. He mused. This job was supposed to be a walkover, even though he had his doubts.

Johnson walked to the window to avoid making eye contact with Stella. He knew she’d have a look in her eyes, the look that she had when she desired him, the look he'll miss when things would properly end between them. She had gotten him all worked up. But it wasn't from what she had just done on the sofa. It was that she'd compare him with another man, that man.

"Oh, I'm calm," Stella murmured amorously, laid back and parted her legs and winked at the lawyer. "I'm always calm, right, JJ?"

"About the papers..."

Stella hummed and undid her dress.

Johnson leaned on the window, brooding. He had all but given up on Kelechi, and for what? For a woman to whom he was second best? Stella had never loved him. She just loved winning and didn't care for who she'd pull down to get there. He rammed his hands back into his pockets and closed his eyes to hold back tears.

Why did he never notice this? Why did it hurt so much? It's not like he loved her. Or had he been in denial all this time? If she didn't sign the papers in normal circumstances, would he forgive her? Never! He'd always see her boss' hands groping her.

"I'll not sign them until I get what I want!" Stella gave the lawyer a cold stare, then her voice turned amorous. "JJ, you make love to me and... well we can't call it making love or love making, can we? No, we'll have sex and I'll give you what your heart desires." She giggled. "Time is running out dear husband of mine."

Johnson arched his back, glanced at her, and returned to his former pose.

The lawyer sighed and went to his document file and pulled a square envelope and handed it to her. "Before you proceed, you may want to take a look at this."

"Very well." She took it and brushed the lawyer's hand lightly.

He frowned at his hand, blinked, withdrew it, and waited. When she didn't move, he gestured and grimaced. He would be stooping this low again.

Stella sighed and opened the envelope to find a CD and slotted it into the drive of her husband's laptop. Then the laptop went off. She shrugged and went back to sit down.

"When you're done, we can discuss -"

She waved her hand carelessly. "There is nothing to discuss. I want a baby, you're giving me one."

"How?" Johnson asked, aghast.

"How else? By fucking me," she murmured, laughed, and slowly untied the belt of her dress, again.

"What the hell?" Johnson growled as he turned to face her.

The lawyer was already standing between them

and turned to face him with a warning glare.

"He wants a divorce, right?"

"Yes." The lawyer calmly retorted, still staring at Johnson.

Stella pursed her lips as she crossed her arms and said, "I want a baby."

Johnson kissed his teeth and squinted at her. All those nights when she had to travel with her boss. All those late hours at work. And Maurice? What on earth did she see in Maurice? He could sort of understand her continuing her affair with her boss since they had already been dating in university. But Maurice?

Johnson returned to the window and leaned on it. He'd given Stella the benefit of his trust, and the person who had needed it was the wife he'd abandoned. Whom, should she have cheated, would entirely be his fault.

"Ma'am, we may want to take a look at the details of this transaction." The lawyer's clipped tone broke the silence.

Unsettled and unsatisfied, she cried. "Enough already!" She leaned forward, connected the charger, and restarted the laptop. "Satisfied?" she asked the lawyer, not waiting for his response, she went to stand beside Johnson. "You've got nothing to lose, you know."

Johnson sniggered.

The lawyer coughed. "Sign it and -"

“Na-aah!” Stella said sharply, wiggling a solitary finger.

“Ma’am?”

“I need my own lawyer too, don’t you think?”

“Perhaps, Ma’am. You’ll sign after the deed, and if you don’t, we’ll share that titbit with your favourite newspaper,” the lawyer gestured, his eyes cold. He needed money, not the drama he was forced to endure. She was getting in the way of his payment, and he could no longer stand it.

“What titbit?”

The lawyer gestured.

“What is so important about the darn CD?”

Neither man spoke a word.

She typed in Johnson’s password and smiled, realising that he hadn’t changed his password. She got up to leave when she heard moaning. She looked at the screen and gasped.

“You didn’t think we’d sit on this, did you?”

She shut her eyes, pained and with a frown murmured, “A good girl knows when to accept defeat.”

“Do excuse me,” The lawyer said in a more jovial tone and nodded at Johnson.

Johnson shook his head. His phone beeped. He wanted to ignore it, then noticed the lawyer’s details on the handle and wondered why he needed to do that. He opened it. It read:

I don't want her coming up with duress in her defence.
I can't be there to make her sign it.
Do what you can.
Good luck!

CHAPTER 29

Kelechi got on the bus heading to Northwood in a bid to visit Simisola and Áyò but got off and decided to take a long walk home. She called Áyò to make an excuse and was glad to leave a message. Another call came through with a number she didn't recognise.

Cautiously curious, she asked. "Hello?"

"It's me. Please don't hang up!"

"Igoni?"

"Yes?"

"Why did you change your phone? What happened to your voice? Do you have a cold?"

"I didn't change my phone. I just wasn't sure you'd want to talk to me. My voice is just fine."

Kelechi chuckled. "So, you decided to change your number. What if I cut this call now?"

"Please don't!"

"Geez, calm down," she murmured, a little worried.

"Did you just say, 'geez'?"

Kelechi chuckled. "I did. Mh-huh, you're the reason. You're a bad influence."

"Glad to be of help."

"So?" she asked, twisting her lips and admitting to herself that it was easier to talk to him via phone.

"Ramsey Nouah is in town for a movie premiere."

"Okay," she drawled, puzzled.

"You don't seem overjoyed," Igoni grumbled.

"Should I be?" she smiled, realising that he would be scratching his head now.

"It's Ramsey Nouah. *The* Ramsey Nouah?"

"Yes, you said he's in town."

"Wow! You're a first!"

She frowned. "Hmm?"

"Most girls would have jumped to the highest heavens on getting a chance to meet Ramsey Nouah."

"Yey! Ramsey Nouah!" she drawled. "Is that better?"

"Yeah," Igoni chuckled. "After bruising my ego."

Wearing an amused smile, Kelechi asked. "Did you have one?"

"Oh, my heart is so broken right now."

"Go and repair it o!"

"Only you can," he murmured, his voice serious.

Kelechi took a deep breath. "I'm out of radar, get it?" she asked in an attempt to diffuse the tension that was beginning to build up.

"Nope."

"I've still got to work on my one-liners."

"Don't see it as a job."

"I'll try." *Too much stage fright to even try.*

There was a short pause.

"I'm going to miss us," Igoni sighed.

Kelechi nodded. "Me too. Stay in touch?"

Igoni in a firm, assertive voice, muttered, "Always."

"Igoni?" her tone was a plea.

He let out a long sigh. "Alright. Whenever you need me, I've got your back. Oh, dear, I'll have to take this call. I'll call you in the morning?"

"Yeah, sure," she murmured, a little disappointed, but shrugged it off as selfish.

"Okay. Laters!"

She heard the phone click and then there was silence.

She had always known silence, at least until she crossed over to England to meet her husband. The silence at this moment felt like torture. It wasn't boring. No. it was just bland, bleak, strange. She looked at the time and back at the road. No longer in the mood for a long walk, she made her way back to the closest bus stop.

Back in the house, Johnson stared at Stella with displeasure at the fact that she had a hold on him.

Stella cajoled playfully. "Why are you acting weird? This isn't your first time with me. Come on, come on, come on."

Johnson reprimanded himself for desiring her.

"It can't be that hard, babe," Stella mumbled and played with her hair. "I'm so horny. I just have to please myself a second time."

Johnson was relieved that Kelechi was no longer in their midst. He'd been concerned about how she was handling all that was happening and was so lost in thought that he didn't notice Stella return to stand beside him.

The corner of her lips twitched into a smile as she cooed into his ear. "I lied, you know. No one has made me feel quite like you do," she murmured and let out an exaggerated sigh. "I'll sign the fucking papers as soon as you make me feel you inside me once more."

Johnson raised a brow at her; she sounded so sincere he was tempted to believe her, but her previous words still hurt.

"JJ, this has gone on long enough. You might as well get it over and done with," she said seriously, clapped her hands cheerfully then asked, "So?"

Johnson slanted his head but remained where he was.

Stella slowly sank onto the sofa, suddenly drained, tired of fighting. She picked the papers and smoothed her hands over them for a while then turned to appraise him. Biting her lips, she scribbled on the dotted lines without reading them and closed her eyes.

"Done, now, your turn," she gestured, but when he didn't move, she waddle towards him, wrapped her arms around him for a few seconds then pulled out his shirt belt. She could feel his lack of enthusiasm to meet her demands, but unhinged, she shrugged out of her dress again and smiled. She wanted to keep him distracted long enough to explain the situation to him and crossed her fingers in the hope that he'll understand.

Johnson unfolded the sofa bed and slowly undid the buttons of his shirt; his heart, crashing against his ribcage as he prayed to whatever god was merciful enough to keep his wife away while he desecrated their union yet again. The yearning he used to have for Stella had drastically waned after he saw the video, and he wondered how Kelechi was able to look at him with such awe after he'd been with Stella.

Looking at Stella, he realised that he missed her. Yet, an ominous string pulled at his heart, and it made him wonder if things would ever really end between them. His trepidation irked him; the fact that he still desired her even though a part of him – a large part – could still see her boss grope her like he owned her.

While they were at it, Henry Hopkins walked in. Johnson had slanted his head, seen him, and decided to stop, but remembering Stella's narration of how he'd touched her, became determined to make her cry out his name the way she always did so he tilted her in a way that she wouldn't see Henry as she loudly expressed her pleasure. The more she pleaded, the more he offered, so much so that she shuddered long after they'd stopped.

Stella planted kisses all over his face, her face tear stricken. He returned her kisses, his eyes on Henry Hopkins the whole time.

"Best sex ever! Can we go again?"

Johnson got off her and went to the kitchen.

Stella let out a satisfied sigh, stretched languidly, then turned to her side opening her eyes. Seeing Henry Hopkin's flushed pained face, she gasped and quickly rolled off the bed. "I...."

Henry Hopkins raised a hand. "Get dressed! We need to talk."

Enthusiastically, she threw on her jersey dress and approached him with outstretched arms. But he shoved a piece of paper at her. She caught it before it fell, scrutinised it, and chuckled. "It can't be!"

Johnson was on his way out of the kitchen when he heard what she said and hung back, waiting for more.

"Apparently, we got married in Las Vegas. How is that even possible?" he asked, his face wrinkled.

"Oh," Stella smirked. She had thought her goodwill ended with losing Johnson. Even in her wildest dreams, it would never have given her ownership of Henry Hopkins, *the* Henry Hopkins she'd always wanted, desired, needed, loved. The one man she thought she would never get over, the same man she thought of when she was with Johnson. Now, she had all the wealth she needed at her fingertips.

"Oh?" Henry Hopkins asked enraged.

Stella shrugged. Remembering how desperately his grandfather wanted one of his grandchildren to give him a greatgrandchild made her angry for not using protection with Johnson. She was ovulating and wanted to get pregnant to spite Kelechi.

"Why did you never bring this up?" he asked impatiently, pacing around her.

Stella was oblivious to the question. She was trying to find out if she had any emergency contraceptive tucked away somewhere; she'd learned to hide them when Johnson was desperate to have kids once upon a time.

"My wife has threatened to sue me for –"

"My wife," Stella spat. "You dare to call her that in my presence now?"

"That's what she is," he said, nodding.

"And that's what I am too," she retorted in staccato, glaring at him.

"Come on, you can't be serious," he muttered nervously. "Do you even care about the repercussion of this?"

"You remember when I fell pregnant just before we went to the US. You said if I were to abort it, you'd marry me?"

"I must have been drunk out of mind to forget something of this scale."

Stella sighed and tried to whittle her anger as she remembered how violent their fights could get. "I didn't know it was valid, or I wouldn't have made JJ marry me."

Baffled, Henry Hopkins asked, "whose JJ?"

"Johnson," Stella muttered nonchalantly.

Henry Hopkins clenched his fist, held his breath, and gritted his teeth simultaneously.

Stella saw his face and understood his pain. It was what she'd lived with until she decided to marry Johnson. She walked to him and caressed him, her hand lingering at his crotch. "I know how it feels. At least you can imagine how I feel when you go back to Otis," Stella paused and chuckled. "whose marriage to you is a farce."

Henry Hopkins sneered. "You seem to forget, we're both bigamists."

"I've signed the divorce papers," she retorted defiantly.

"What? You think that's enough?"

Stella wrinkled her nose and quickly bent over the paper. "My marriage to you is legitimate, yours to her isn't, the same rule applies here. I'll leave you to dwell on that. In the meantime, I got somewhere to be," Stella licked his face, then winked at him as she sauntered out of the house.

"Stella! This isn't the end of this discussion." Henry Hopkins bellowed as he went after her.

Johnson heard the door and stopped the recording. He hoped his lawyer would have some use for it. He thought of Kelechi and quickly tidied up. Hearing the click of the keys, he gathered his things and ran into the bathroom, then frowned, wondering how Henry Hopkins managed to get into the house without a key.

Kelechi entered the house giggling.

"He must be very big now o! I still remember his loose teeth. Oh my goodness, he was always misplacing his teeth. Oh, I'm fine," Kelechi muttered.

She thought she heard something and spun. With a hand to her chest, she shook her head in a bid to shake off the memory of Stella's indecency. Failing, she sighed ruefully.

"I just remembered something I forgot to do. Okay, that'll be nice," she feigned cheerfully and ended the call.

Relieved, she tucked the phone in her pocket. She was always glad to hear about other people's bundles of joy, but it forced her to keep a brave face or smile until her face ached for fear that she didn't remember to smile. Walking past the bedroom, she tried to avoid looking at the sofa, but it wouldn't let her be even the stench lingered.

It would always serve as a reminder of how formidable Stella was, a woman of guts while she remained the timid people-pleaser. The one thing that dragged her into England, she couldn't even bring herself to do it. How hard could it be to get pregnant? She couldn't achieve the one decision that she'd made. She was healthy and medically speaking, without flaws.

She raised her brow at the pile of clothes in the corner of the room then wrinkled her nose. She'd abandoned washing for so long she was out of clean clothes. The house was too quiet; she looked around, still trying to avoid the sitting area in the living room. Opting to wash everything, including the ones she had on - there was no one else in the house; Stella had moved, and Johnson would likely return late. A little detached to the world within the walls of the building she'd somewhat gotten trapped in and in an attempt to cling to world she had once known, she wore her earpiece and turned up the volume of the music, but not before securing the latch to keep the outside world at bay. She sauntered, danced, and cleaned the house, including the sofabed.

Johnson came out of the loo to find her giggling again; her face was so animated that he almost forgot the reason he'd rushed into the bathroom. He quickly picked up his boxers and tiptoed back to the bathroom. At the door, he paused and chanced a look at his wife, but she didn't seem to notice him; he wondered if it was a good thing not to worry.

He was alarmed to hear his wife's raised voice. It was the first time he'd heard her sing and was surprised that she was tone-deaf. He smiled, shaking his head; she even made cleaning look sexy. Watching her shimmy aroused him so he got rid of his clothes and made his way to her dancing.

As soon as his hands touched her, she jumped, screamed, and scrambled away from him.

He stifled a chuckle as she scowled at him. A frown briefly appeared on his face as he stood his ground, not willing to let her keep him out.

"What on earth is wrong with you?" she asked as she tossed a dishcloth-cum-rag at him.

"I'm sorry," he raised his hand to fend off the offending extension of her hand.

"I'm sorry," he reluctantly murmured. As she

shuddered violently, he remembered what Maurice had done and how his action may have frightened her.

"Nwunye'm, I'm so, so sorry. I didn't realise... I..."

He cautiously approached her. Unsure of how to bring her comfort, he stalled. He was so close, his hand eager to help, but he didn't know how to handle her new stance. He watched her scrub her neck as if her airway had been clogged by a formidable force. For some reason, she sobbed as she fought off an invisible hand. Baffled at the fact that there were no tears in her eyes, even as she whimpered, he stood awkwardly beside her then hovered for a while.

Finally, he came to kneel beside her and gently pulled her into his arms, massaging her back and murmuring into her ear. He inclined his head to take a whiff of her scent and sighed in agony; she smelled of orange and lime.

He stroked her face, still murmuring gentle words. She tilted her head up, pulled away briefly, and cupped his face, only hesitating for a few seconds before planting a kiss on his lips.

He hungrily reciprocated.

CHAPTER 30

At 6AM on the dot, there was a knock on the door just as the alarm of Johnson's phone tore through the serene quietness of the room. It was too early in the morning to be having guests, so they ignored the door. Johnson reached out to stop the alarm and then rolled over to pull his wife to himself. The knocking increased and then stopped. Kelechi groggily roused and went to the bathroom, too lazy to turn on the light.

Another knock, more rapid and forceful, made Johnson sit up. Remembering Stella, he decided to ignore it, willing her to get lost.

"It's the police! Open up!"

Kelechi wasn't sure of what she'd heard and wished she had not flushed the loo at the same time. She turned and was about to make her way out of the bathroom when she heard a loud crash. She suspected it was the door, the draught that came in confirmed it.

Seeing that she was as stark as the day she was born, she ran behind the door just as someone pushed it open. She sucked and held her breath, standing on her toes. A torchlight trailed around the bathroom, but because of the crooked space behind the door, she wasn't seen. The owner of the light switched it off and closed the door, but she remained there, afraid to move, afraid to leave.

The tightening in her chest made her struggle to breath. Something was obstructing her airway, something she couldn't see. She scratched her throat, but it wouldn't let up. She fell to the ground, still struggling, she clawed at the ground looking for a grip.

"Get dressed lad!" A new voice cried.

Johnson shook his head in disbelief.

"You're under arrest on suspicion of fraud and bigamy."

Johnson blinked, getting up. *It was too soon.*

He stumbled forward. One of the policemen blocked his path. Feeling dizzy, he began to mutter; none of them seemed to be listening. He could hear another one talk, and he tried to gesture, but they held his hand. He tried to explain, but they glared sternly at him. He suspected that it was because he sounded like he was gargling water.

One had already pulled out his taser, and another with hands on his belt, parted his legs.

The one that was talking rolled his eyes and reiterated what he'd said earlier slowly, but Johnson simply blinked at him.

"You've heard what this man has said, haven't you?" a tall man, the only one with hair on his head, asked, walking towards him.

The curtain was drawn, making Johnson wince.

"Are you alright, Sir?" the tall man asked.

Johnson tilted his head away from the light and turned his head the opposite way, trying to get rid of the water in his ears even though he didn't remember submerging his head in water.

The first man spoke again. "Mr Johnson Umeh, I'm going to arrest you on suspicion of fraud and bigamy. You understand?" He asked and beckoned another police officer. "You do not have to say anything. But it may harm your defence if you do not mention when questioned something which you may later rely on in court. Anything you do say may be given in evidence."

Johnson looked around, alarmed, worried, and defeated. His heart raced much faster than a few seconds ago, and it felt like he'd just received a blow to his chest and bent down, desperate to sit down just as they were about to slip on the handcuffs. His action seemed to have invoked the attention of the other policemen because the next second, they were wrestling him to the ground. He tried to protest, but he only made it worse as they took their vendetta on his wrists.

Johnson was surprised and dazed because he'd never been in a fight - much less gotten into trouble and didn't know what real pain was. The pain was excruciating, but he didn't have anything to compare it to. He didn't know his limbs could be twisted in that manner, and it eased the tension that he'd had in his back for a long time.

"What..." he started and stopped, mostly from disbelief that he could hear himself.

"We're going to take you to the police station where we'll interview you in relation to this matter, alright?"

Kelechi struggled to catch her breath. She'd never been so scared; she'd never had a reason to be this close to the police or witnessed an arrest. It was a new experience, another dishevelling, unsettling, and unwelcome experience.

As soon as her breathing returned to normal, she retched. For an unfathomable reason, she stared at her gut-mess until the smell filled her nostrils. The shock, the pain, and alarm topped anything she'd ever felt. This was worse than the first time she came across Stella; perhaps because the former simmered and seared while this was swift like a cut from a razor blade and scorched like the accidental spill of hot water but inside the skin.

It was like coming to be with her husband was a test of what she could take in body and soul. It had been impossible to think clearly since she came into the house. The depths and heights of her roaring emotions scared her because she no longer recognised her feelings and sometimes, herself. She also dreaded the lengths she would go to get what she wanted and doubted she was still on the right track.

She had never been an impulsive person. She was Kelechi Owhornuogu, the uncompromising and diligent go-getter. She never rushed into anything, always had a contingency plan, even for the most minute indulgences. She always achieved her goals at her own pace, slow and steady.

Absentmindedly, she sauntered into the bedroom then paused to stare at her fingers. She realised that she hadn't bitten them in a while.

Does this mean that I've grown more mature these harrowing months? Or I'm neither sad nor happy? What should I be feeling? I'm still my old self, am I not? Is it wrong to believe in the sanctity of marriage?

She shuddered at the thought of almost giving herself to Igoni. She had felt no shame or regret. Whatever the test was, she wasn't sure she'd pass them because she desired her husband more even now.

"The Bible gives me the right to divorce my cheating husband! What does it say about the man never apologizing? What does it say about a woman who went back and still considers a divorce? Can I safely say I'll not hunger for a man's touch the way I yearn for my husband's touch?" Kelechi moaned. "I should be focused on my coming exams. Jesus, your path is difficult!"

A knock on the door brushed off her thoughts; her phone rang in tandem. Picking it, she ran back to the bathroom. She didn't remember changing it to silent mode but was glad that it was. The knock became more persistent, but she was neatly tucked behind the bathroom door like she was earlier then swiped it when it rang again.

"Hello?" she asked in a loud whisper.

"Cousin, do you have a cold?"

The comfort of hearing a familiar voice calmed her frayed nerve that she almost forgot to respond. "No, it's just hard to –"

"Bad time eh? Let me call when you're less busy or call me back."

"No! Please don't hang up!" Kelechi exclaimed and covered her mouth. Tears streamed down her face, unsure if they were borne from relief, defeat or a defiant realisation that she was still alive.

"Stay where you are, I'm coming!"

She sighed when the phone went dead. Not wanting him to stay longer than necessary or get involved in the ensuing drama, she decided to pack a bag. As soon as she was out of the bathroom, there was another knock. For some reason, she felt a crippling fear that threatened to paralyse her. Her heart had skipped so much for one day. Realising that the door had not been fixed, she decided to take a look through the bedroom window. It was the man that returned with Johnson last night.

"Who is it?"

"Mrs Umeh, it's your husband's lawyer."

She frowned; she hadn't realised that her husband had a lawyer. She opened the door to let him in and thought against it, but it was too late; he was in the hallway. She looked surreptitiously for something close by that she could use to defend herself.

"The police have taken him," she murmured.

"This isn't looking good," the lawyer groaned, then mopped his head with the handkerchief that was quite discoloured.

She raised a brow at him as she waited for his next line of action.

He continued mumbling to himself as he vigorously scratched his head. It was so smooth that she was concerned with his injuring himself. When he finally stopped, his head was as red as a strawberry.

It made her wonder. *Is it an itch or a habit? Is that what I'm doing to myself? Am I mutilating myself for an itch? What is my itch? Fear. Of what? Maybe the need to stay married? No, I think it's something else! Could fear sponsor duty? How does it work?*

"Mrs Umeh," a dull voice called.

She flinched when something touched her. Looking up, she remembered the lawyer. She frowned at his hand on her shoulder, and he removed it.

"Mrs Umeh, would you like me to contact someone on your behalf?

Kelechi tilted her head away, wondering what he meant, and her eyes fell on the paintings. "The painting," she mumbled. She'd forgotten about them.

Someone else knocked. The knock was more like a thump that the door came crashing down. Kelechi's heart beat so wildly that the light that flooded in made her assumed she'd died and gone to heaven.

"Who are you?" Johnson's lawyer asked.

"Who is he?" her cousin brushed past the lawyer and stood by her.

"Jay's lawyer," she gestured. "Barinem, my cousin."

"Oh, I see," Barinem looked at the lawyer

briefly as he said, “Kechi, get your things.”

Kelechi didn’t move. The paintings, something about them called to her, but she couldn’t figure out what it was. When she didn’t budge, Barinem entered the room, picked up the first bag he saw, and began to dump things that he suspected were hers in it. Then he pulled her up, but she shrugged him off.

Worried, Barinem asked. “What is it?”

“The paintings.”

“Paintings?” The lawyer asked, curious this time.

Barinem followed her gaze and pulled off the drape to reveal the paintings. “Could you assist me, please?”

“Of course,” the lawyer said frowning, and then squeezed past Kelechi.

As they carried the final painting out, a picture fell. It was the likeness of Stella but with knock-knees and much darker red hair. The people behind her were black, the woman sitting down had a huge afro hair and carried a baby in her arms. The red-haired girl seemed happy. The face of the man in the picture was smudged. There was an older woman behind the couple who didn’t smile. Sighing, she picked it up and left the room. In the hallway, she tucked it in the bag her cousin had packed and went out after them, then returned to lock the bedroom door.

Something about the picture bugged her.

CHAPTER 31

In Barinem's hotel room, Kelechi played with the remote control, not realising that she'd missed a few calls until the phone fell with a thud. She didn't know how she managed to sit through her exams with her inability to concentrate. It had been five weeks and counting since Johnson's arrest. There were lots of reporters waiting for her or Stella to appear therefore she couldn't visit Johnson, nor did she desire to.

"Hello?"

"I'm from the –"

She groaned and ended the call. "These people are quite resourceful, *sha*," She grumbled and roused, saw a newspaper in the bin, and took it out, shaking her head. "How can they hope to protect me from this?" she sighed and opened it, her face was plastered on the front cover with the caption: *The Bigamist's Wife*.

Kelechi snickered. "What do they know?"

She carried it back to bed and began to read with a scowl. The first sentence of the article asked: what woman would let her husband bring home another wife?

"What woman indeed?" she sighed and read the article halfway through and screamed, "I didn't have a choice!"

Defeated, she began to cry and promised not to read anymore. After a while, she read it all and other ones. 'They had proof of her mental stability', one had said. 'She was timid, in support of what her husband was doing', another said. 'They cooked up the plan together', 'she was suffering from domestic violence', 'she was even the mastermind and shouldn't go scot-free because no woman in her right mind would share her husband except unaware of the woman'.

Burnt Oak had become too small a hiding place as her life had become a filmmaking street, and she wished it was fiction. That way, she would go to bed, and it would all disappear when she opened her eyes to the real world.

It didn't help that she fell asleep at intervals. For some reason, she'd been unable to stay awake for longer than an hour for the past two weeks; coffee had no effect, and her body grew weaker each passing day. She'd passed out a few times. She could no longer keep up the charade when she passed out in the bathroom to the shock and amazement of Barinem's fiancée, Nadine – she'd never seen or heard someone passing out in a sitting position.

Kelechi knew the phrase *media attention*; she just didn't realise what it felt like. She was a simple girl who wanted to lead a simple life. Her only ambition was to be a good wife and a great mother. Now, her life was a publicity stunt. She'd had to change her phone number twice because of the request for interviews.

She shuddered as she remembered the first time she'd encountered them. It was when her husband was called before the court. She froze, staring at the disorientating flashes and shadows. Unfortunately, these shadows were not phantoms of her imaginations. These ones were real, they probed, interjected, accused, bruised, and swashed her. And here she was, thinking that poking on Facebook was condescending. Fortunately, Barinem whisked her into his car, into a cab and another cab for fear that they would trail her.

The bigamy charge she understood, but the fraud and theft by false pretence didn't fit; a part of her wanted to witness the proceedings, but he and her cousin would not hear of it, at least until the letter arrived. Staying in her cousin's room was confining, mainly because she couldn't put her hands to good use.

She pondered about the courthouses; she'd already been called to be a witness in her husband's case. She had a feeling she was going to start hating Wednesdays.

The lawyer suspected there was an underlying reason, but she didn't care. All she wanted was to see Maurice go down for laying his hands on her. Underlying or not, she also wanted to prove her sanity to herself and wondered if her walking on a straight line was enough proof.

Morning came hungrily on her court day.

In the court, she felt like a cattle drawn to the slaughterhouse, a cattle that seem to have given up on life. Her clanking court shoes reminded her of her racing heartbeat. No matter how hard she tried to calm her nervous heart, it followed the composed rhythm of her shoes. Maurice's lawyer sneered her contempt.

She'd been prepped about the proceedings but willed it to pass quickly, all the judging eyes and questions demanded her soul and yet determined as she was, she couldn't bear it. It was like an underlying force held her tongue in forceps, daring and taunting her. She silently pleaded for help as Maurice's lawyer made her guilt a requisite for shame just because she didn't cry out for help until the landlord knocked on the door.

As she stepped out of the constrictive witness box, she frowned.

Did I in anyway beguile Maurice? Would I have let him have his way? Was his success the required evidence?

As the questioned fleeted through her thoughts, one of them obsessively returned until she asked. “Why didn’t I object?”

“Fear!” a voice spoke from behind the lawyer.

Kelechi looked up, startled; she didn’t realise she’d asked out loud. She frowned hesitantly at the woman through blurry vision, unable to make out who understood how she felt. She was, however, not interested in the racket that ensued or the bang of the gavel behind her. Her interest was in knowing why she was afraid to react the one time she needed to.

Before she got married, if anyone as much as touched her inappropriately, she would fling something at them.

Outside the courtroom, she sat down and sighed. *I’ve changed a lot this year, but for better or worse?*

“May I?” A woman sat down beside her before she could answer. “You know, I’m angry and sad and happy, is that not weird?”

Kelechi raised a brow briefly at the woman and looked away.

The woman sat up and continued. “I’m angry that he’d embarrassed me this way. I’m sad because of the woman I’ve become because of him, a bitter unsatisfied woman. I’m happy because I’ve found my voice again through you.

Thanks for that!" the woman got up, smoothed her hand on her clothes, and walked away.

Kelechi pursed her lips. She'd been trying to blow off steam but held it all in to keep prying eyes at bay.

"What did she want?" The prosecutor asked when he finally joined her.

She appraised him for a while and then lowered her head.

"Jemison!" the lawyer for the defence called and came to join them, then shook hands with the prosecutor. "Yesterday's case was a willy wonka."

"Speak for yourself," Jemison retorted and chuckled.

Kelechi appraised the defence lawyer who seemed to be doing the same. Her eyes were too small for Kelechi to make anything out, not that she could. Yet, she questioned what lay in the defence lawyer's eyes. Pity? Contempt? Or a snide silent rebuke?

Kelechi watched them dilly-dally in frozen conversation, and something with human legs blocked the comforting sunrays that would have gone unnoticed but for the interference.

"You've succeeded, you witch!"

She didn't need to raise her head to know it was Maurice's mother. She was in anguish again. Everyone accused her. First, it was the prosecutor of Johnson's case who'd accused her of fraud not long after her husband's lawyer had asked her to annul their marriage, and then the court accused her of trapping her husband by refusing to grant him a divorce to be with the woman he loved. Then her mother-in-law accused her of sending her son to prison.

Now, this woman was accusing her of sending her son to prison, like it was her fault that the woman didn't bring up her son properly. It was a sheer stroke of luck that they now had evidence that Stella was equally married to a prominent man who was also married. The media not wanting to be left out, pointed more accusing fingers.

Kelechi got up and briskly walked towards the exit. As if on cue, the lawyers followed.

The woman went after her and tugged her around. "By the time I'm done with you..."

The media circus cut the woman off. Kelechi had forgotten about them. Closing her eyes, she could shut out the flashing lights but not the noise. Her chest tightened, and she was overwhelmed with the desire to make them vanish, so she screamed at the top of her lungs.

Everyone's first reaction was absolute silence; then, everything went agog. The cameramen and their counterparts were in a frenzy, the defence lawyer stumbled backwards, shaking her head and rubbing her ear, the prosecutor collected his briefcase and nudged her in a different direction. She frowned and pulled back, wondering where the bubble had come from, then staggered. She fell fast with nothing to grasp on until everything went black.

Kelechi opened her eyes to find Igoni staring at her.

"Wow! See who's returned from the dead!"

"Igoni?" she inquired weakly.

"One and only. Babe, you wan kill me?" Igoni asked, cupping her face.

"Wetin happen?" Kelechi asked, wrinkling her nose.

"I really don't know, but your..."

"You passed out again at the courthouse," Barinem muttered as he adjusted her pillow and replaced Igoni in the chair.

"What?"

"Mh-huh, you've been out for days."

"Days," Kelechi murmured.

"Yes, days." Barinem nodded and glared at Igoni who shrugged defiantly. She wanted to ask about Johnson but felt it wasn't right to ask the men in front of her. As the news was about to start, Igoni quickly changed the channel, and Kelechi smiled ruefully. Barinem and Igoni getting along was no mystery; she was certain it had everything to do with her and Johnson.

She cried until she fell asleep. Crying was now her favourite past time. She cried so much so that she didn't notice Igoni walk in until he pulled her to himself and rubbed her back as he consoled her. His gesture made her cry even more because it reminded her of her last night with Johnson.

She should feel betrayed, aggrieved, and perhaps vengeful, but she just wanted tranquillity, a sustained composure for her delicate soul. There was only so much a human body should be allowed to endure or withstand.

Johnson was all the family she had when her grandmother passed, which was why she was willing to move in with his parents and wait for his return. It was the reason she endured all his family meted on her. The people who gave her strength were no more as they either faded away or were tucked out of her way like an eclipse.

Kelechi stared at the wall. Tears never came; everything seemed to have taken a languid pace since the case against Johnson was dismissed. It felt like her marriage had been dismissed too as days passed to months. The clarity of how to proceed with her life failed her.

CHAPTER 32

Kelechi stared at the lady across from her, forgetting for a brief moment why she had come to the surgery. A month had passed since the trials ended, headaches replaced her fainting spells so much so that she was asked to come in for blood tests. A few days later, she returned to discuss the result.

Kelechi stared morosely at the doctor. Whatever else he said, escaped her.

"How could it be?" she whispered. *The universe has played yet another trick on me. Why do I always have to be fate's bait, a pawn in their bitter game?* She lowered her eyes and pressed her stomach, then chuckled nervously and looked back at the doctor.

"We could always run another test?" the doctor quipped hopefully.

Kelechi laughed. *What does he take me for? A lab-rat?* Her heart raced with hope, fear, worry, and gradually, she calmed her nerves and nodded.

"This time, we'll do a blood test."

Kelechi raised a suspicious brow.

"Let's eliminate our fears, shall we?"

Kelechi shrugged. She watched the doctor make a call and sighed. She had nothing to lose except perhaps hope. Better not to dwell on it and focus on the excitement of getting a scholarship to continue to her Masters. It would make a good excuse to evade her fears, she thought.

She waddled behind the doctor, followed the nurse, and grimly watched the nurse draw blood from here and pondered on the future result. However, the wait. The wait she had always dreaded. She'd learned the consequence of waiting from her marriage. Perhaps they'd been a tad hasty, but they had nothing but love for each other. She could admit it now. After all she'd been through, she could finally admit to herself that she loved Johnson Thomas Umeh. She'd always known, but it felt good to admit it.

'Was it enough to stay?' she'd been asked. To that, she had no answer as she was still figuring it out.

A gentle breeze met her as she stepped out of the surgery. Sighing, she lifted her head, closed her eyes, and took it in.

"Excuse me," a woman huffed, eyeing her suspiciously.

Squinting, Kelechi stepped out of the woman's path. Heading home, she took a different bus and didn't check the listing until she heard the name of the bus stop: Colindale Avenue; she had retaken the wrong bus as she'd meant to visit the shops in *The Hyde* so she went window shopping. As she turned to the path leading out to the bus stop, she stumbled across a group of spectators and caught sight of her friends: Áyò, Simisola, and Zainab who made a quick exit. Though Áyò and Simisola were curious about the abrupt exit, they were more interested in Kelechi whom they'd had not seen in a long while.

"How are you? How have you been?" Áyò asked after they'd exchanged greetings.

"What would you like?" Simisola asked, getting up.

"Nothing," Áyò mumbled, shaking her head dispassionately as she quickly typed into her phone.

"I'm not asking you jó?"

"I've been there," Kelechi said to Áyò, and shook her head at Simisola, who returned empty-handed.

Áyò frowned at the empty high stool, dropped her phone in her bag and said, "Let's go watch a movie."

"Áyò! I'm tired of the way you change your mind at will. Is it not you that said you wanted to go home and rest?" Simisola groaned then turned to Kelechi. "That's what she's been doing all day. I didn't get to finish buying what I needed for the bridal shower."

"Bridal shower?" Kelechi asked before she could stop herself.

"Yes, oh! My neighbour's daughter. The woman is housebound, so I'm helping her out," Simisola sipped her drink and glared at Áyò.

"Why don't you go ahead -" Kelechi murmured and rose from her chair.

"And leave you to yourself? I think not!" Simisola shook her head.

"Well," Áyò smoothed the skirt of her dress. "I'll go home if we're doing nothing else."

Simisola snorted and pondered. "Aright, why don't I stay here while you two go and fetch me a pink veil?"

Kelechi shook her head.

Áyò scoffed.

Simisola sighed dramatically, "wait for me then."

As soon as Simisola was well away, Áyò took a peek at the contents of Simisola's shopping bags and giggled.

"Don't do that!" Kelechi admonished.

"Why not? She does it to me all the time."

Kelechi turned to the sound of yelping children. It reminded her of the doctor's words, and she wanted to share the news but thought it wiser to wait.

"Are you okay?" Áyò asked, looking concerned

as she pulled her chair closer to Kelechi's. "How have you been?"

"So so," Kelechi retorted, looking at the back of her hand. "You?"

"That's not an answer abeg! Are you sure you don't want something to drink? The coconut-banana smoothie is heavenly."

Kelechi shrugged, conceding. It did sound heavenly but a treat from Áyò she didn't relish. She frowned at the crowd's rhythmic humdrum and wondered why people were so different and so in sync at the same time. Feeling defeated for acknowledging the fact that she could no longer hide her worries, she sighed.

"Here we go," Áyò mumbled and gingerly stretched her hand to Kelechi.

"So, tell me for real, what's going on?"

"Nothing."

"Nothing? How can you say nothing? Where is your husband? How is he? How are you coping?"

Kelechi arched her back defiantly. She hated Q and As of this kind, more so after the court cases.

"Fine," Áyò moaned. "I know you'll prefer to express yourself to Simi, it's fine... I should be used to it by now."

"No, it's not that o!" Kelechi grimaced. "I've not yet seen Johnson because I've been staying with my cousin," she paused and quickly added, "to avoid the media, of course."

Áyò sighed. “It's a lot to take in, but I’m glad that's over sha.”

Kelechi gulped accidentally. “You are?”

“Before nkó! The media just twist everything. I’m glad you and Barinem and Igoni are... Where *is* lgoni?”

“How am I supposed to know? Oh my god, you sef! All you had to do is ask about lgoni instead of beating around the bush.”

Áyò pouted. “I’m over him!”

Kelechi scoffed playfully. “Indeed.”

“He isn’t over you,” Áyò said quietly.

“I noticed,” Kelechi sniggered, she should have known that Simisola would spill. She couldn’t let Igoni be close anymore. What would be the point? He’ll only end up being hurt. The distance would be good for her too. Safer.

“Will you move on with him?” Áyò drawled as she tried to conceal her curiosity.

“Of course not!” Kelechi almost shouted.

Startled, Áyò leaned back to create space between them. “Aa-ah! No be fight nawh!”

“Sorry,” Kelechi apologized. “I'm a little exhausted.”

“It must be the sun,” Áyò offered.

“It must be,” Kelechi agreed and quickly sipped the smoothie Áyò had ordered for her to bridle her tongue. Áyò was not the best person to pour one’s heart to, and she was now desperate more than ever to do just that.

"Do you still love him?"

"Love who?" Kelechi asked, idly.

"Your husband!" Áyò scoffed.

"I don't know!" Kelechi said through gritted teeth. She didn't want to be asked the question she'd been avoiding, trying to trade, the one question that she'd tucked away for fear of admitting the truth. None of them understood why she still loved him. She didn't either. More so, she didn't understand why they still asked the same question.

"Oya o! Let's go!" Simisola returned empty-handed.

"Wetin hapun?" Kelechi asked, getting up though concerned.

Áyò frowned at her, not budging.

"I don't know yet - the school just called."

Relieved that they were well on their way to leave her to her thoughts, she helped Simisola carry some of her shopping.

CHAPTER 33

Kelechi was quiet through the journey; a question plagued her – would she really go back to him after all that had transpired?

Simisola drove past a shop, and she knew they were in Burnt Oak, she saw but took no notice. Watling Avenue, in the flat above a betting shop, the first place she'd lived with Johnson as a couple, but with another woman who'd first to play that role. Thinking of it made her spite herself.

She hadn't been back since her husband's arrest. Being back reminded her of questions like, did he love her? Did he just say those three words to get her to sleep with him? With Johnson, it was hard to tell. She was married to him for nine years, known him three years before that, and lived with him for just over one year, and she didn't know what he cared about.

She did have a glimpse once. She smiled as she reminisced.

He'd made an unplanned trip back home. His university had been shut down due to a riot that had gotten out of hand. It had been her best year because they got to see each other unhindered. The source of her pain, his mother, had gone to her niece who'd just delivered a baby. It was on one of those days that she decided that if he ever asked for her hand in marriage, she was going to accept it.

January 14th, 2007. It was also the day of her grandmother's memorial. They'd just returned from Mass, and he didn't want her to stay at home, so they took a bus heading to Buguma to visit the beach. He wanted to prove to her that Kono was a water-front and not a beach. He succeeded. She stood still on the fine tan sands, speculatively eyeing the endless azure waters.

"The world is a big place o!" she'd whispered, mesmerized.

"It is indeed," Johnson had said and wrapped his arms around her, but she'd wiggled out of it, fearing what she'd let him do if she stayed. Suspecting he would be offended by it, stretched her hand to him. He took it, and they walked along with the receding tide.

Johnson scratched his head. "Do you think you would ever leave your grandmother's house? What I'm trying to ask is, would you like to travel the world?"

"I don't know. Why?" she asked and stopped to pick a smooth stone.

"Nothing," Johnson shrugged.

"Nothing abi?" She had given him her most incredulous look. "So, you brought it up because you thought it was nothing?

"My mother..." he started and paused.

"She's seen another way to keep us apart," she'd countered, annoyed and not wanting him to continue. He was blind to his mother's tyranny.

"You know that's not true. She's just a woman who's trying to protect her only son."

"Mh-huh, from a local champion," she retorted, unable to stop the sting from coming through, but he didn't seem to notice.

He chuckled. "Are you not a local champion?"

She'd balled her fists and looked up at his playful smirk and relaxed. He'd meant it as a joke. "So, what did you discuss about me?"

Johnson shook his head and turned her to face him, "That I want you to rule our world."

"Eh!?"

"By my side," he nudged her and continued, "As soon as I graduate and get a job, we'll move to Port Harcourt. There, you'll take JAMB, enter the university, graduate, then the world becomes our oyster."

"I don't need the world, TJ," she had said, shaking her head because she didn't want to get sucked into his dreaming.

"Don't we all?" he asked, bemused.

"And we can't all be you," she finished and tugged her hand out of his.

"Of course not! Not all can be as lucky as I am."

She stopped walking again and frowned at him. "I don't understand."

"You complete me. Do you know how hard it is to find the one person that's compatible with you?"

"Simple English, please?"

He'd cupped her face briefly. "You're my world."

Kelechi shook her head and scoffed.

"Nwunye'm," Johnson said so softly she barely heard it.

"You have no right to call me that!" She'd almost shouted, alarmed and elated. Her lips twitched to the side as she tried to hide her excitement.

"Why not?" Johnson has asked, standing very still, his arms spread like he did when he was confused.

"You've not paid my dowry nawh?"

Johnson dropped his hands and raised a brow at her. "Is that all?"

"Don't be dismissive. Paying my dowry gives you rights. Rights that are very far from you let me tell you now," she'd said, clicking her fingers for effect.

Johnson stopped and quickly pulled her to him in a tight embrace then leaned in to kiss her, but she turned just in time for him to plant a kiss on her cheek. He smiled, let her go and turned away.

Kelechi bit her lip. "You're angry."

"No, I'm just finding it hard to endure... to wait."

"Be strong," she cooed, patting him on the back.

"Don't do that," he grumbled.

"Do what?"

"That thing you do and call it encouragement. You're not in my shoes."

"I've always been in your shoes. You just haven't taken the time to notice," she murmured, shaking her head as she strolled on.

Johnson waited a while then joined her. "I'm sorry, that was selfish of me."

"Will you always care?" she finally asked after a long silence.

"That's an odd question sha!"

"You never answer sha!" she retorted, mimicking him.

"Why wouldn't I?" Johnson frowned, suspecting it was a trick question.

She shook her head again and stared at the wild waves ahead.

Johnson was quiet the rest of the time.

She ate in silence. Her thought reverting to the

advice her mother had given her: 'you should never be the other woman'. She was eight at the time. It had happened after she got into a fight with her best friend over who would sit beside the new boy in school. In their fight, she ruined her only uniform. As punishment, she was made to wear it to school for two weeks, which incurred more punishments from her teachers.

Then her mother made her a cake, as white as a sunny day cloud and as soft as butter. That day she learned of a brother who had died a few years before she was born. Also, that her father had a wife before her mother, making her mother, the other woman. Her mother had looked forlorn in the candlelight as she narrated the story.

"I had married your father to spite my parents. There's nothing they didn't do to stop it. They had kicked against my first two choices. I was stubborn and I was angry, so was my father, but the desire to get back at them for making me lose the love of my life prompted me to accept your father and therefore had to abandon home for England to be with him.

The problem began a few months after we'd arrived; there was always something to fix at the other woman's room. The fixing only ever occurred at night and was never finished. I wasn't a child. I asked questions and got the beating of my life, which resulted in my losing the baby, a few weeks before I was due. We had to bury him in the garden at the back of the house.

The only other person who knew I was in the house was the midwife, Samaira. Samaira was an illegal immigrant, a dainty woman who always smiled, even when people were rude to her. It was later that I realised she couldn't read or understand most of what people said.

I also discovered to my amazement that the woman in the other room wasn't a relative, but his first wife, his legitimate wife, and I was to be their baby factory. The plan was for me to have a baby or two, then they'd kick me out when I'd weaned them. With nothing on my back except the clothes I had on, I left the house. I walked for miles until I was too exhausted to carry my weight.

It was then that I came across some people living on the street in cardboard boxes. They were having intelligent conversations. There, it dawned on me that I had to come up with a plan, but I was no planner, so I went to visit the only other person I knew, Samaira. She gave me contraceptives and told me to come over when my husband and his first wife left for work.

It was through her that I met a former police officer, Sergeant Colin' O'Sullivan. He taught arts and crafts to little children. I went to help out when Samaira couldn't. He saw my interest and introduced me to his sister, who was housebound. Through his sister, I learned to set the table, to bake, and all about catering.

Two years had gradually gone by, and the guilt of being the second wife or the other woman waned. But the longer it took for me to get pregnant, the more resentful the first wife was. The more time he'd spent with me, the more resentful she became.

One day, via my carelessness, she found my contraceptives, but then careless enough to leave it where she found them, I took them away and returned to my duties. From then on, I carried them everywhere I went. After that incident, I knew I had to concede. Besides, my lessons were almost over.

Following Samaira's advice, I never practiced my skills or any knowledge I acquired in the house. I, with the help of Samaira, registered for antenatal care. When my husband discovered this, he told his wife, and from then on, when I had an appointment, she would go with me.

Then one day, the first wife had a conference which was to last a week and, of course, didn't want her husband to be with me, so they left together. It was all Samaira needed; she induced labour, and I had you. Sergeant O'Sullivan had already got my flight ticket and gave me an envelope which had a letter and money in it. With £80, a suitcase full of children's clothes, and a box of cooking and baking utensils, I returned to Nigeria. Your grandmother welcomed me. Your grandfather couldn't object because he'd had a stroke. It was then that I realised I could do so much with so little.

Your father was still in my life because of you. I quite frankly couldn't see myself with another man. Besides, I wanted you to have some stability.

If that new boy likes you, he'll come for you. I'm telling you from experience. If his heart is not with you from the beginning, what makes you think it will be with you in the end? Nothing. You may have something that he desires, but his heart will be where it will be. Well, what I'm trying to say in essence is, you should never be the other woman.

Now Dear, fetch me a plate so we can devour this cake."

It was the last time she'd seen her mother; her parents died that night.

Sighing, Kelechi wiped her eyes.

"AW!" Kelechi shouted and raised her hand to ward off the offender.

Áyò glared suspiciously at her. "Girl, you sure sey your head set well?"

"What do you mean?" Kelechi asked, blinking.

Simisola observed her.

"Do you know how long we've been calling you?" Áyò asked, scowling.

Kelechi raised a brow, shook her head, and sighed. "I'm sorry, I was just thinking of the other woman."

Áyò and Simisola looked at each other and shrugged.

Kelechi got out of the car and frowned. "Why are we here?"

"Oti o! This girl don kolo!" Áyò exclaimed and raised her hands to her head.

"Get a grip on yourself," Simisola rebuked Áyò and touched Kelechi gently. "We're at your house."

"Oh no, I've moved."

Simisola frowned briefly and sighed. "Okay, tell us where so we can drop you."

Áyò tapped Simisola in disagreement, and at the same time made furtive glances at Kelechi.

CHAPTER 34

Kelechi smiled and even giggled properly for the first time in a long time; it had been such a long time since she thought about her mother. Memories of her mother used to hurt, but lately, it's been a source of relief, sometimes comfort. She smoothed her hand over the picture that had initially bugged her for a while. She was curious to know who the paintings belonged to, but the landlord didn't know as lots of tenants had passed through his house. She would have loved to know the people with her parents in the picture.

"What's up?" Barinem asked, walking into the living room.

"Oh, just remembering Momsie," she murmured and stretched.

Barinem staggered to a halt. "What did you say?"

"You heard what she said," Barinem's fiancée retorted, brushed past him as she made her way to Kelechi. "Tell me about her."

Kelechi did, Barinem narrated the memories he had too and then Kelechi showed her the picture that was attached to one of the paintings.

"Nadine Shaw!" Barinem's fiancée exclaimed. "I'm named after her."

Kelechi tried to take the picture off her, but Nadine had already reached Barinem and was poking it.

Barinem took the picture and laughed long and hard then said, "Small world. This is my aunt, her husband. I don't know the rest."

"This is my nan and her mother," Nadine explained excitedly.

Barinem's eyes bulged. "Your grandmother is black? How did that happen?"

Barinem's fiancée nudged him playfully. "She was adopted."

Barinem feigned disappointment, and his fiancée jovially wrapped her arms around him.

Kelechi shook her head at him, smiling.

Barinem looked adoringly at Nadine. "Did you think we would come this far?" Barinem asked.

Nadine chuckled and smothered him with kisses.

Kelechi snickered. Her cousin's words took her back to a time someone had used those exact words.

As the sun began to set, they packed to leave the beach. Johnson stopped and turned her to face him. Thinking he wanted to kiss her, she slanted her head away shyly. Johnson took off his leather bracelet. He took her hand and pushed it gently onto her wrist.

"I may not have a ring to give you right now, but I give you my heart and hope it's enough to swing the tides in my favour."

Appalled at first, then shocked because she knew how much the leather bracelet meant to him, she stared at him. It was a gift he'd retained his entire life from his best friend, his great grandmother. She never took it off, except when she gave it to an Aboki to fill grain, tan, and glaze it.

"Promise me one thing?" She had asked. "No matter how bad things get, you'll tell me the truth."

"Always. Promise you'll do the same?"

"Always," She replied softly, looking at her feet for a long time and then said. "You must promise me that if I ever turn out to be the bad wife of a good man, you'll stay by my side until my head is set right."

"Vice versa. But why would I need to turn you around? You can do that all by yourself. You're the best thing that has happened to me, so when I forget, you'll remind me in more ways than one."

She broke a branch off a dwarf tree and wrinkled her face as she asked, "How's that possible?"

"We're one. No matter how far I get, that signal will bring me home."

"Your homing beacon," she murmured and sighed as her heart threatened to explode, then nodded, pride welling in her.

"I think we've been watching too many sci-fi movies," he sniggered and rested an arm on her shoulder.

"It's your fault," she defended, letting his arm rest on her shoulder for a while then wiggled away.

"Eh?" he interjected. "Is it not you that said it's the best way to study the sciences?"

"Well," She reiterated and nervously played with her hair.

"What?" Johnson inclined his head.

She lowered her head and, in a low voice, said, "I want you to kiss me."

He froze; he hoped she wasn't taunting him.

She frowned just as he leaned in and kissed her.

Kelechi sighed and squinted at the sudden brightness. The light had been turned on.

"We dey comot o!" Nadine said, shyly.

Kelechi chuckled.

"I did good, right?" Nadine asked with a crooked smile.

Kelechi nodded, even though she was tempted to tell Nadine she was trying too hard but smiled sweetly. "Have fun."

"Will you be okay on your own?" Barinem asked.

"I resemble pikin?" Kelechi asked sternly.

"Point taken," Barinem said coolly. "Rest easy, see you later."

As soon as they left, Kelechi went to the kitchen to get the cookies she'd saved and scooped out some ice-cream to go with it when she heard the door. Thinking they'd forgotten something, she stared at the bowl; it was too late to retreat, so she came out with it. The shock of seeing *the* unexpected guest caused the bowl to slip from her hand, the sound of the clatter didn't startle her, but the coldness of the ice-cream on her foot did.

Johnson was already on his knees, pleading. "I'm sorry! I thought you approved when I first heard that you were cheating on me. I didn't believe it until I received your letter. For days, it hurt I thought it was punishment for my cheating on you, I was sure I could fix our financial problems if I stayed a little longer. Then it became increasingly difficult to cope. When your letter came, I said well, it's not like you've been faithful. You didn't want anything to do with me anymore, so I married Stella."

Kelechi blinked back tears, remembering. *It's partly my fault. I just wanted the noise to stop; your mother's incessant insults, your cousins' constant bullying that when Maurice promised to let me be, I agreed to write it for him. I didn't see him keeping his promise, but I had to hope.* She became suspicious when, after writing the letter, he asked her to sign it. It didn't seem right. And though asking her to sign triggered alarm signals, her desire was for him to disappear was more.

"I will not lie to you; I cared about her, but she wasn't you. No one could replace you. I grew more fond of her, then I thought, I've got a job, a woman by my side, soon children will come. what was the point of going back to start over?"

Kelechi wrinkled her nose.

"And then you came. I was even more confused when you gave yourself to me untouched and wondered why you would let me be with another woman as a wife and not a side-chick."

Kelechi rolled her eyes contemptuously, wondering why she was still listening to him. She decided to savour seeing her husband on his knees and sat down.

"I was torn between you and Stella because she is a good person just as much as you are, and a part of me felt it would be easier if I alienated both of you from each other. But you don't know how to hold a grudge, and sooner or later, the truth will out. But I've never made to any woman the promises I made you, the promise I intend to keep. I didn't leave her because there was another man. I only waited to have an excuse to leave. I know I didn't need an excuse, but I wanted one to be justified in my actions.

But she would only give me a divorce if I slept with her. I didn't know she would tell the police. I don't even know how she got to know."

Kelechi sighed again. *What do I want now? A lot had changed after writing that letter. The day I wrote the letter for Maurice, was the same day I moved back to her grandmother's house, but your father fell ill, and I moved back in despite Father Jude warning me to leave for my sanity.*

"Everything just went wrong from there. I couldn't protect you. I found out that none of the letters I sent you got to you and went to ask Maurice how he got your letter if he gave you none. He said he'd pretended to have broken his hands and needed someone honest to write a letter for him."

What would my life have been if Father Jude had not intervened? Would I have seen the four walls of a university? Would I have gotten my HND? Would I have been here?

"Nwunye'm, if I had known I would never... I would have been back home a long time ago. You're my girl from home. You're my euphoria. I could never forget that. Forgive me and come back. Please, you're all I've got. You're all I need,"

Johnson stopped and began to rock himself, pleading.

Kelechi swallowed and grimaced as she remembered what she'd been through with her husband's insane family. A burden she took on because she loved a man who was the only family she had until she discovered that her cousin Barinem was alive. But, she wanted stability and couldn't decide what it would be. She still hadn't figured out what his feelings for her were. For all she knew, he could have come to plead with her because Stella had gone to Henry.

"Nwunye'm, you're not saying anything," Johnson complained.

"I'm the one that called the police on you," Kelechi replied so quietly that Johnson almost missed it.

Johnson choked, sat on the floor, nursing his knees, and stammered. "What?"

"Yes, I needed to know what you wanted with me. You weren't saying anything. I had made a choice when I left Naija to be with you, my husband, have your kids, and live happily ever after. After my discovery, I thought perhaps I'll take in and go back until you were financially buoyant. I mean, I wasn't getting any younger." Kelechi let out an exasperated sigh and frowned. "I hadn't expected to find another woman in my place."

“Nwunye’m,” Johnson started.

Kelechi scoffed and waved him off nonchalantly. “To come to you, I had to sell my grandmother’s house so I would have had nothing to go back to, and there was no way I was going to go back to your parents' house. Prison would be better than that any day.”

“But Nwunye’m,” Johnson murmured and moved towards her.

“See, how easy you say it as if you know what it means?” She yawned, bored with talking but still carried on. “Unlike you, I believe in the sanctity of marriage. Being with Igoni made me realise I cannot be you and how determined I am of not being like you.” She paused for a while, shook her head, and continued. “Up until now, I didn't think I had a voice. I thought it was the marriage, the man, the children that made the woman, but that’s not it. It’s what she makes of herself. I never understood my mother’s stories until now. Her advice when I was only eight has kept me going, and I didn’t realise it. The truth is you don’t own me. I know that now.”

“But, I never did,” he countered, frowning.

“Hush, I'm still talking,” she admonished.

“Can I get up?”

Kelechi glared at him. "Where was I? Yes, I’m no longer going to fuss over you. I’m loyal, not stupid. You want me back, and I get it. But I have a few conditions."

Johnson nodded eagerly.

Kelechi went away and returned with a large envelope and a pen.

He took it from her.

"Sign them, please."

Johnson looked downcast.

It's now or never. "Sign it, Johnson Thomas Umeh," Kelechi retorted, surprised that she was able to keep her voice even.

Johnson, eyes blurry, gave her what she wished for her freedom. He wished she could punish him in a way that they'd be together until she healed.

"You signed it?" Kelechi asked, shocked.

"That's what you wanted," he murmured.

"I see," she perused and frowned though somewhat relieved. "Why? That's not a signature!"

"I'll never divorce you!" Johnson affirmed. He wanted to get up but remained on the floor, not knowing why.

"Why?"

"Because I love you."

"I see," She retorted, her heart blossomed even as she tried to keep a straight face. She'd waited for this answer for a long time but, how else could she test him?

"No, you don't." Johnson scrubbed his face. "As I.. long as I breathe, I'll fight to be with you. I promised."

Kelechi scoffed. "You didn't keep your promise, why now?"

"I did, but there was a mix-up." Johnson pointed at a knapsack. "May I?"

Kelechi nodded.

Johnson produced the letters Maurice's wife had posted and handed it to her.

Kelechi read them but showed no expression. It didn't make a difference; she knew what she wanted. There was no guarantee that Johnson wouldn't cheat on her again. Moreover, she was more comfortable knowing that he wasn't flawless. She let out a deliberate sigh and dramatically laid the letters on the island. "My conditions."

Johnson looked hopeful.

"You'll sever your ties with your family; we'll remarry and start afresh. Your journey of wooing me begins today. As soon as I graduate, we're going back to Nigeria. We'll live in Lagos. If you should visit any member of your family, that day, our marriage is over."

Johnson nodded. He wasn't keen on going back to Nigeria or severing family ties but hoped he'd have time to convince her otherwise.

"Why aren't you angry at me?"

"Angry? About what?"

"That I called the police."

"I was relieved. The pressure to keep up the charade was driving me mad. I'm just glad that I didn't end up in prison. I don't think I would ever forgive you if I did."

Kelechi turned to face him squarely. "I'm not sorry." Smiling, she added, "Welcome home. I'll always be your homing beacon. Be careful sha!"

"Why?" Johnson asked, his frown deepening.

"Because your homing beacon can also be the trap that sends you to an early grave."

Johnson chuckled and raised an amused brow at her. "How can I?"

Kelechi smiled ruefully and kissed him.

Johnson reciprocated hungrily.

Kelechi pushed him away and undressed.

Johnson became suspicious, wondering why she was undressing in her cousin's living room, especially after what she said about an early grave. He became even more alarmed when she started kissing him again and undressing him roughly.

"Nwunye'm, maybe we should hold off, " he urged nervously.

"I'm on heat right now! You don't want to piss me off," she snapped.

"Ah! I... eh. Mmm. Why don't we just take a deep breath?"

Kelechi scowled at him as she fidgeted with the hook of her bra.

"Don't worry. I just realised that I've got a

husband to mend," Kelechi mumbled and smiled mischievously as she let the dress drop to the ground.

Johnson stifled a groan. Fear crowned his hesitation, and hunger curbed it. "Nwunye'm," Johnson drawled.

"Now, now, kiss me quick," Kelechi smacked her lips and undid the buttons of his shirt.

"With all pleasure," Johnson murmured.

A few minutes passed, then Kelechi stopped abruptly and got off her husband. "I'm hungry."

Johnson watched her walk away and blinked. As she had never abandoned him high and dry and their reconciliation was still in its early stage, he suspected she was punishing him. He groaned and mourned as he looked below his abdomen. Sighing, he went to meet her in the kitchen, hoping to convince her to change tactics.

Kelechi moaned as she devoured the melted dessert.

Johnson wrapped his arms around his wife and kissed her. Her continuous moaning made him hungrier, but his hunger was of a different kind.

Kelechi moaned as Johnson smooched her and patted her legs. As soon as he did, she said: "JJ, don't cheat on me again."

"Never," Johnson murmured; his voice laced with his arousal.

"Mmm," Kelechi kissed her teeth. "You'll not

like to know the consequence." She shoved him off her and stretched. "I don't think I want to continue."

Johnson exclaimed and cried. "Kelechi, see me nawh!"

"What?" Kelechi turned around, looking confused.

Johnson gestured.

"Oh," she frowned. "So? Do you know how many times I had to go to bed desiring you and getting nothing? Abeg eh, go and take a bath, you'll feel better."

Johnson froze.

Kelechi grimaced as she said, "I feel so hot all of a sudden."

Johnson gave Kelechi an incredulous look. "Nwunye'm, abeg, I don't like this joke o. Are you going to leave me like this? For real?"

"Oh no, I just don't feel like it," Kelechi retorted then peered at the floor near him with a disapproving shake of the head. "You're dripping on the floor."

Johnson blinked. This was the worst kind of torture. It wasn't the type he was likely to survive. He took her hand and led her back to the sitting room after she prepared a second helping of dessert with only one intention – to seduce her.

"Nwunye'm, is everything okay?"

"Why won't everything be okay? I'm only

pregnant. Do you have a problem with it?" she asked, glaring at him.

"What? No! Of course not! Not at all!" He was surprised; a part of him had doubts about its paternity, but he didn't mind.

Kelechi observed her husband. She found it weird that she felt turned on and suddenly didn't. She hoped it wasn't because she still had some animosity towards him. His return and his declaration of love didn't give her the satisfaction she'd hoped for. There was something missing, something she needed but couldn't place her hands on. She had no fear of his being a good father, but there was a doubt that was wedged somewhere in her thought. Something that reminded her that it wasn't enough for him to profess his love to her.

Sighing, she stretched her legs. *I must be the most confused person in the world right now.* However, she was hungry. Her appetite had doubled, and her interest in food had dwindled with its growth.

She hurried back to the kitchen, opened the fridge, and stood in front of it for a while. Nothing piqued her interest, so she went to the cupboard. She browsed through the kitchen cabinets, but nothing appealed to her except ice-cream and cookies. Tempting as it was, this was going to be the third bowl, albeit the first one was on the ground.

Johnson's phone began to ring and irritated by the offending sound, Kelechi called Johnson to get it. A few more times, and Kelechi screamed his name.

"Pick it nawh! I'm in the toilet," Johnson retorted.

Quite irritated, she picked the phone and before she could welcome the caller, she heard: "I know you don't want to hear anything I've got to say, but I'm pregnant, it's yours, and I'm not doing this by myself."

Kelechi gasped.

Zainab!

She shook her head, gesturing.

JJ, Zainab, it can't be!

"Hello? Are you there?" Zainab asked from the other end of the phone.

CHAPTER 35

Kelechi withdrew the phone from her ear slowly and set it down far from her reach.

Zainab and my husband. How? When?

Kelechi scratched her head, trying to figure out why she hadn't noticed, how she could have missed it, or why she didn't suspect. Nothing made sense. Yet it did - Zainab's desire to be her best friend, calling to visit at odd hours, bringing her food knowing full well that she could cook.

She'd expected an affair with full-frontal Áyò but had stopped the intrusion when she caught Áyò ogling her husband. If Stella had come back to say she was pregnant, she'd believe it because she'd seen them together and never found leftover protection. Even as she expected it, she dreaded it.

Zainab and Johnson. Who initiated it? Johnson, of course! Zainab was not so bold, acting like she owned the world and as sneaky as a rat. But why on earth would Johnson, with everything going on, still want to frolic with another woman, a married one at that? Was he that depraved? Did I marry a demoralised man?

"Were I and Stella not satisfying him?"

"Who's him?" Johnson asked.

Kelechi didn't know when he came out of the toilet. She just stared morosely at him, her mind reeling with questions as she tried to make sense of the man she'd entered into a marital pact with. She may have promised to be his homing beacon, but at this rate, it would be better that he was lost at sea.

"Who are you, really?" Kelechi whispered.

Johnson frowned. The phone was not in her hand, and he wondered who had called so he could defend himself.

Kelechi shook her head vehemently as she clicked her fingers in disgust. "You're not the man I married."

"Hiah! Nwunye'm, what is it? What happened? Are you okay?"

"Yes o! I'm very okay," Kelechi retorted in Ikwerre language.

Johnson knew then that he was in big trouble. She used to resort to Pidgeon English, but ever since she met Stella, she expressed her displeasure in Ikwerre language.

"Doorbell. Get the door," Kelechi gestured. She watched him go and returned to clicking her fingers, still baffled.

Johnson barely finished unlocking the door,

when someone pushed the door into his face. He bent down to nurse his bleeding nose with a yelp.

His cry drew Kelechi's attention. She laughed sarcastically, clapping her hand. "The rain fell, and he brought the mud in with him."

Johnson frowned and straightened. "What?"

"So, this is where you chose to hide," Stella murmured as she appraised the house, her weekend bag swaying with her.

Johnson barely had time to react to Stella's appearance when Zainab walked in.

"I have come so we can talk," Zainab muttered and crossed her arms, rolling her eyes at Johnson.

Johnson's heart hit the floor, but he wasn't going to let her mess things up for him. Determined, Johnson raised a questioning brow. "Sorry, were you talking to me?"

"No! I'm soliloquizing!" Zainab clucked her tongue.

Barely acknowledging her presence, he turned his attention to Stella. "Why are you here?"

Stella unhooked her bag, sat down, and began to type into her phone. "I'm here to discuss an important issue. It involves your duty as a father."

It was Johnson's turn to be sarcastic. "What?"

"I'm pregnant!" Stella sighed and looked expectantly at him.

Johnson chuckled. "Sorry?"

Kelechi gave Johnson a brief condescending

look and turned to Stella. "So, you're pregnant for Johnson." Then she turned to Zainab. "And you're pregnant too, for Johnson."

Stella squeaked, staring at Zainab, who simply shrugged.

"Indeed, you're a man!" Kelechi said in Ikwerre language, shaking her fist, snickering.

Johnson jumped over the couch and rushed to Kelechi's side. With his forefinger, he touched the ground, his tongue, and raised it up. "Nwunye'm I swear! I have nothing to do with that woman o!"

"Say what you have to say in a language I understand, abeg!" Zainab muttered, avoiding Kelechi's gaze.

"See me see wahala! Have I ever been with you?" Johnson asked Zainab as he gestured to his wife. "I told you o. Remember when she tried to seduce me, see."

Kelechi frowned and studied her husband. He wore a straight face usually. When he didn't, he had disgust written all over it.

"You're not even his type," Stella defended then frowned in doubt.

Johnson nodded in agreement while his eyes pleaded with Kelechi.

Zainab chuckled. "Does he even have a type? My dear, we've been at it since the day you travelled. You even saw me when you returned."

"Nwunye'm, I swear, true to my Heavenly

Father, I haven't. You know I'll never lie to you."

"I've got proof o!" Zainab snorted.

"I want to see it," Stella said and turned to face Zainab.

Zainab hesitated. Their transaction had always been cash-based. "We dealt with cash only. Check his account for these amounts on these dates." She produced a long sheet of paper from her purse.

Kelechi withdrew from them, preferring to watch from the sidelines at a safe distance where she could cower in shame.

"No way! No one is going through my account!"

Stella giggled. "Then it's true. You're indeed a dog."

"I'm not! No one is going through my account!"

CHAPTER 36

"Johnson Thomas Umeh, open your account," Kelechi quietly ordered.

"Nwunye'm, don't do this. You know me. They are lying, oh! Believe me, I haven't slept with her, I never have!"

"Please, do it now," Kelechi whispered, shakily climbed the stool, her hands held the sides of it in a firm grip, then she bit her lip and lowered her head.

Feigning reluctance, Johnson opened his account and mumbled. "Nwunye'm, it's because of you oh!" He knew this day would come when Zainab would come to collect. He knew she'd do anything to keep him on a leash. But he was prepared; he'd been prepared from the first day.

"There's nothing there," Stella, who'd been worried, was now hopeful and played with her hair.

"You lie," Zainab continued, determined. "He must have another account."

"He doesn't. I checked," Stella mumble, suddenly exhausted. "See for yourself. I knew everything he owned."

Kelechi gritted her teeth at the burning sensation in her chest.

"Kelechi, I don't know the game you and your husband are playing, but I'll not take this road alone o!" Zainab spoke hastily and pointed at Stella. "You can bear me witness."

"Witness to what?" Stella asked, confused. "I thought you had a husband."

Zainab kissed her teeth. "Kelechi, talk to your husband - I'll not take care of this child on my own o!"

"Nwunye'm," Johnson went on his knees again. He sighed, blinking back the desire to make love to his wife as he remembered that she was wearing nothing underneath her long shirt-dress. She'd resisted him; he'd been thinking of seducing her until she succumbed before these relentless women showed up. They just didn't know when to stop. The devil is a liar! Imagine, their audacity, just as he had made amends. When his blessing was about to be complete, the vipers appear. *It will not happen!*

"Nwunye'm, you know me. I'll never lie to you. Stella was a mistake, babe. I've never seen any other woman's nakedness since we got married." He lowered his head, holding onto her legs. As he made that statement, the women all flashed through his memory, their judging eyes, even the shame in Portia's eyes. Then he averted his gaze for fear that his eyes would betray him.

It was all before I married, Stella though, he amended in his thought. Zainab was just a means to an end. She should go back to her husband and stop chasing another woman's husband. He belonged to his Nwunye'm, his one and only Kechi.

"I'll describe his penis," Zainab mumbled, licking her lips.

Kelechi winced.

Stella looked on anxiously.

Johnson flinched then buried his head in between Kelechi's legs.

"He's slightly bent when rigid, and it has a narrow reddish-brown birthmark near the tip, just along the edge." It was Zainab's turn to cringe and turn away - she had described Johnson's landlord's.

Stella was the first and only person to laugh.

CHAPTER 37

Kelechi stifled her excitement. She had willed her eyes to shed no tear and her heart to turn to steel. She had seen the desperation in Zainab's eyes and was convinced that something had happened between them. Her head no longer hung low from fear of shame but from the embarrassing guilt of believing Zainab, for letting her doubts in his ability to be faithful cloud her judgement.

"I guess it's just you and I then," Stella said and sauntered towards Kelechi, but Johnson blocked her path. "didn't know you missed me that much." She puckered her mouth and leaned forward. "Oh JJ, I miss you too," she murmured, resting her hands on his chest.

Kelechi placed her hands on Stella's and said matter-of-factly, "State your case."

"Oh well," Stella withdrew her hands, shrugged, then sauntered back to the sofa. "I want Johnson back at least until the baby is born. I'm going to be the mother of his child. You can accord me that."

"Really?" Johnson asked and scoffed.

Kelechi glared at him. “So, Stella, what then happens to me?”

Stella shrugged. “Don't know, don't care! You can be there like you used to be, invisible.”

“Did she say invincible?” Kelechi asked.

“Yes,” Johnson said quickly with a frown, wondering what Kelechi was up to.

“I said invisible,” Stella emphasized and spelt it. “Anyway, it doesn't matter. Even if JJ feels tied to you, it will only be a matter of time before he realises his mistake.” Stella sucked her teeth and added, “only a matter of time.”

“What then happens to Henry Hopkins?”

Stella’s face turned pale.

“What about Henry Hopkins? How is he going to handle this little fiasco? Surely he knows what you're about to do?”

Stella raised a brow at Kelechi, her attempt at being imposing. “What is it to you?”

“What Johnson is to me,” Kelechi retorted and shrugged. “You see, I read the news. He is in prison because of you.”

Johnson raised his brows, shocked.

“He has lost his known wife and with it the business partnership because of you. He has lost his father's company because of you. Now you want to take his only child away from him because of you.” Kelechi leaned in and whispered into Stella's ear.

Stella turned red and shied away from her. "But," Stella stammered, "it really is Johnson's."

Johnson laughed nervously. "It's not mine, but after its birth, we can talk shop."

"What he said," Kelechi gestured with a small smile. "With me in the mix, of course."

Zainab had already gone before Stella made her painfully slow exit. Johnson, for the first time in all the events past and present, felt remorseful. He'd almost lost his wife a second time, for papers, for money and then perhaps for babies which hadn't been on the agenda until he learned his wife was pregnant an hour ago.

He had a faint suspicion that both Zainab and Stella's babies belonged to him. This only meant one thing – he had to go back to Nigeria with his wife as soon as possible. He couldn't afford to wait until she was done with her Masters. They'll all have their babies by then. There had to be a way to escape quickly and quietly, which most likely would involve a lot of money.

He saw his phone vibrate and stealthily picked it up as he went to shut the door. It was a text message, and it read:

You know where to find me.

It was from Zainab. Curiosity quickly replaced his grimace as he quickly switched off his phone.

"Nwunye'm!" Johnson called as he returned from shutting the door. When she didn't respond, he bent over the counter to turn on the kettle, saw her phone, switched it off and went to the kitchen to fix them each a cup of hot chocolate; she nodded her thanks when he returned to her side.

She seemed oblivious of him, but she looked happy.

Concerned, he moved to the high stool beside her to keep an eye on her. Just then, the door opened again, and a couple stumbled into the house.

"Guess who I'd just seen?" Nadine squealed before she realised there was someone else in the house. "Is he?"

Kelechi nodded, disinterested.

"Hi, I'm Nadine Shaw! Your wife's soon-to-be sister-in-law."

"Hello," Johnson retorted slowly, his focus on Kelechi.

Barinem hugged his cousin, whispering, "Is he giving you any trouble?"

Kelechi shook her head and sighed.

Barinem, seeing that she wasn't in the mood to talk, pulled his fiancée away, not glancing at Johnson.

Johnson sighed when Barinem looked over his

hand and walked away. He knew he'd have done worse to any man who'd treat his sister with such scorn if he had any. He moaned silently; it was going to be a long rocky road. He looked down at his eager manhood in anguish.

A long rocky road.

He let out a worried sigh and prayed that the journey of endurance would be mapped with little pleasures.

Kelechi couldn't believe herself. A split-second and Stella appeared in front of her, touching her husband in front of her, and something feral reared from within her. In that second, she wanted to be identified as Johnson's wife, Kelechi Johnson Thomas Umeh.

She'd earned it, and she had every right in the world to keep it. She wasn't going to be the other woman in her home. She was going to run it as she deemed fit.

Who knew marriage could bring out the best and the worst in me?

Either way, if she ever changed her mind and sought a divorce, she would make him sweat tears as she had done in the past year. She was open to the idea of forgiveness, but she had better things to feed her emotions with, and it wasn't Johnson Thomas Umeh.

She rubbed her stomach as she reminisced.

One thing was certain - she didn't believe she would travel across the world to find her husband, nor that she would ever leave her grandmother's house, yes, she did. The world was indeed her oyster, and she'll mould it into what she wanted it to be.

Once upon a time, she let her world revolve around Johnson. She was the girl from home who hid in the gaze and shadow of her husband, but no longer. It was going to be all about her. She looked at her not yet bulging stomach and smiled. Zainab and Stella had come to shame her, but little did they know; she would let them believe that until it was time, until it was time to show the world that this girl from home, came, saw and conquered.

Naivety had indeed waned.

ACKNOWLEDGEMENTS

I'm indebted to HRH Louisa I. Ezinwo who has been my best friend, hero, favourite critique and mother.

You gave me the best motive – 'give and make it the best it can be'.

A special thank you to Adaoma, Niki, Celia, Felicia, Chinyere and Tochitony who helped spin the wheels of this plot.

Also, by Agnes Kay-E

Rhythm of the Wild Drum and Other Stories

Tainted Hearts

Agnes Kay-E
Nicholas'
First
NATIVITY

As Kemka Ezinwo

Something New

Also, by the Author as Kemka Ezinwo

Captured Within

Like me on Facebook:
https://www.facebook.com/AGNKayE

www.ingramcontent.com/pod-product-compliance
Lightning Source LLC
Chambersburg PA
CBHW030333310726
48979CB00001B/14

* 9 7 8 1 9 1 6 3 7 1 0 0 2 *